the
ultimate
film
guides

Se7en

Director
David Fincher

Note by Nick Lacey

Longman

York Press

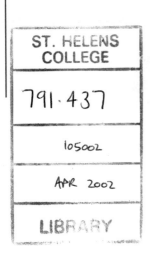
York Press
322 Old Brompton Road, London SW5 9JH

Pearson Education Limited
Edinburgh Gate, Harlow, Essex CM20 2JE, United Kingdom
Associated companies, branches and representatives throughout
the world

First published 2001

ISBN 0-582-45257-0

Designed by Vicki Pacey
Phototypeset by Gem Graphics, Trenance, Mawgan Porth, Cornwall
Colour reproduction and film output by Spectrum Colour

contents

For my students

---///---

author of this note   Nick Lacey graduated from
Warwick University in Film/Literature and has been teaching Media
Studies since 1990. He is a contributing editor to *in the picture* and
author of a series of advanced level Media Studies textbooks for
Palgrave: *Image and Representation* (1998), *Narrative and Genre* (2000)
and *Media Institutions and Audiences* (2001). The British Film Institute
published his *Film as Product in Contemporary Hollywood* (with Roy
Stafford, 2000). He is also the author of the *Blade Runner* York Film Note.

background

trailer

'Seven', a dark, grisly, horrifying and intelligent thriller, may be too disturbing for many people, I imagine, although if you can bear to watch it you will see filmmaking of a high order ... 'Seven' is unique in one detail of its construction; it brings the killer onscreen with half an hour to go, and gives him a speaking role. Instead of being simply the quarry in a chase, he is revealed as a twisted but articulate antagonist, who has devised a horrible plan for concluding his sermon. (The actor playing the killer is not identified by name in the ads or opening credits, and so I will leave his identity as another of his surprises.)

Roger Ebert, The Chicago Sun-Times, *22 September 1995*

A high-concept serial killer prowls the murk in *Seven*

They bicker and bond – a wise, weary detective (Morgan Freeman) in his last week before retirement and an eager kid (Brad Pitt) fresh from the country and ready to kick some big-city butt. Police partnerships don't come any lower concept than this. On the other hand, the serial killer they are pursuing, a creepy, brainy religious fanatic played by Kevin Spacey, is a high-concept kind of guy: he's trying to commit seven murders in seven days, each of them supposed to illustrate one of the seven deadly sins in some preposterously stomach-churning way.

Luckily, the setting for Seven (the title is the only understated thing about the picture) is an anonymous metropolis where it rains all the time and no one seems to have paid his light bill. The murk hides some (but not all) of the grisly details. Murk is also the auteurial hallmark of director David Fincher (*Alien 3*). Aiming to be a modern-day Bosch, he ends up doing MTV bosh.

RS Time Magazine, *25 September 1995, vol. 146 No. 13*

buckets of bloody vomit

> Fincher has created the most authentically hellish screen metropolis since Gotham City, a nameless warren of damp corridors, subterranean sex joints and dilapidated tenements, where it rains all the time ... [the film] stands as the most complex and disturbing entry in the serial killer genre since *Manhunter*.
>
> *John Wrathall,* Sight and Sound, *vol. 6 issue 1, January 1996*

> 'Seven', a grisly social allegory drawn in blood and spawned in despair, casts a lingering, malodorous spell. A buddy-cop thriller recast as Dante's sojourn in Hell, this graphic, allusion-littered film stands the conventions of the genre on end – along with the viewer's hair. Sitting through it, if God is just, should count as penance for our sins – including Thomas Aquinas's seven deadly no-nos ... Sometimes the film is so murky, you have to wonder: Is it art, or did Fincher just forget to pay the electric bill?
>
> This is a blessing, though, for viewers repelled by cockroaches feasting on cadavers and buckets of bloody vomit. These filmmakers are unflinching in their macabre vision. 'Seven' leaves little to the imagination. Fittingly, there are warnings along the way that the viewer's patience and sympathy will not be repaid. Somerset, the weary stoic as played by Freeman, comes straight out with it: 'This isn't going to have a happy ending. It's not possible.'
>
> *Rita Kempley, Washington Post Staff Writer, 22 September 1995*

reading se7en

Once upon a time, a young idealistic cop, and his wife, move to the big city because he thinks he can do some good. He's teamed with a cynical partner who is about to retire. Together they seek a serial killer who is using the Seven Deadly Sins as his inspiration. The killer is captured and the young cop, and his wife, live happily ever after.

Imagine *Se7en* concluding in such a way, something studio executives desired. The film would have remained stylish, exciting and depressing

a European sensibility

but, crucially, audiences would have been let off the hook at the end. Fortunately we have *Se7en* as it is, a film of contradictions: downbeat ending but popular; entertaining and bleak; genre and art house; European and American.

Virtually all Hollywood narratives are structured as fairy tales and so offer a happy ending. *Se7en* managed to be both subversive in its ending – people do not live 'happily ever after' – and popular: it grossed over $100 million at the North American (USA and Canada) box office.

The downbeat ending (to understate the case) is not entirely absent in Hollywood's output, indeed during the 'New Hollywood' of the early 1970s it was not exceptional (*The Godfather*, 1971, for example). However after *Jaws* (1975), the High Concept (see Contexts: Hollywood) 'summer blockbuster' became the studios' preferred method of making money and films conceived as blockbusters generally do not have unhappy endings.

Most people watch Hollywood cinema in order to be entertained. The biggest box office films of the year are invariably 'popcorn movies' whose ambition is to do no more than make money by entertaining as many people as possible. In North America, the world's biggest market, recent top grossing movies have included: *Independence Day* (1996); *Titanic* (1997); *Armageddon* (1998); *Star Wars: The Phantom Menace* (1999) and *Dr Seuss's How the Grinch Stole Christmas* (2000). With the exception of *Titanic*, which dealt with social class and gender, these films have little, or no, pretensions about making significant statements about the human condition. *Se7en*, on the other hand, offers a vision that is bleak with virtually no possibility of redemption.

Se7en, like most entertaining films, is a genre movie; or rather a mix of a number of genres including film noir, serial killer and horror. It is also, in many ways, an art movie where ideas predominate over visceral pleasure. In this it has a European sensibility rather an optimistic brashness that typifies North American product. Despite this, all its main creative personnel, cinematographer aside, are American.

Many deride Hollywood for producing formulaic and banal films. This it does, but Hollywood also produces masterpieces like *Se7en*.

key players' biographies

DAVID FINCHER

In recent years, many directors have taken the 'film school' route to Hollywood. After graduation they often make small independently-produced films in the hope of getting noticed by the major studios. Fincher, born in 1962, took a more practical route and started working, in 1980, for George Lucas's Industrial Light and Magic (ILM), a special effects company. He did this for four years before moving on to making television commercials and music videos, which he continued to do in the 1990s.

It is an apprenticeship that suggests an emphasis on entertainment and surface gloss. His films, however, show great craftsmanship and depth (see Director as auteur). His first feature film, *Alien³* (1992) flopped at the box office and evidently was a painful experience for Fincher; studio interference made it a difficult project. *Se7en*'s (1995) big box office (it grossed $250 million in international markets, that is outside of North America) made Fincher a hot name, but neither of his follow-ups have been as commercially successful: in North America *The Game* (1997) grossed $46.4 million and *Fight Club* (1999) $37 million. However, again the international grosses far outweighed the domestic with $61.1 million and £71 million respectively (source: *www.boxofficeguru.com*).

After *Fight Club*, Fincher's next project, *The Panic Room*, was described as 'something a little more conventional' (*www.davidfincher.net/ updates.htm*). Fincher knows that is important to maintain box office credibility in order to get funding for the more 'interesting' films.

BRAD PITT

Brad Pitt was one of the most charismatic stars of the 1990s, though his box office record is not one to inspire undying loyalty from the major film studios. Undying loyalty, however, is something many of his female fans would swear.

He first made a major impact as the roguish J.D. in *Thelma and Louise* (1991) who awakened Thelma sexually and stole her money.

Part of the reason Pitt's box office record is not particularly lustrous is that he is unafraid to take risks in the films he chooses. *Fight Club* (1999), for instance, his second film for David Fincher, is an incredible, surreal *tour de force* ('edgy' in studio parlance) that bemused those in the audience taken in by the appalling marketing campaign that made the film seem to be a macho fist-fighting fest. Offbeat the film certainly was, but this did not stop Pitt taking a $17.5 million pay cheque, a substantial proportion of the $68 million budget. Pitt, however, will take a pay cut to make movies he likes and his presence helped the relatively low-budget *Snatch* (2000) to box office success. He is also not averse to playing unsympathetic characters; in *Seven Years in Tibet* (1997), his Nazi Heinrich Harrer takes a full hour to become a remotely likeable person.

Whilst part of Pitt's onscreen charisma comes from his drop dead good looks, he is undoubtedly also an excellent actor. Pitt's beauty is such that he is often filmed for glamour. In *Legends of the Fall* (1994), it was difficult to decide what to look at: Pitt, with his long locks flowing behind him as he raced on horseback, or the breathtaking Montana Rockies. Here Pitt plays an outsider, alienated for much of the movie from his family and seeking death after he failed to save his brother in the trenches of the First World War. *Legends of the Fall* and *Seven Years in Tibet*, like *Sleepers* (1996), are melodramas and Pitt seems ideally suited to the emoting that features in that genre. In *Sleepers*, he appears constantly on the verge of tears, no doubt adding to his appeal for many female fans.

Pitt offsets his 'feminine' glamour with his muscled body, complete with a six-pack stomach, and his charm is roguish. He is a man of action rather than thought, his Harrer in *Seven Years in Tibet* would not have survived without help from Peter who makes sure he has enough food. With the exception of *Sleepers*, where he plays a lawyer intellectually pulling the strings, Pitt's characters emphasise the physical. In *Se7en*, Mills constantly fidgets (rubbing his hand in his hair), waiting for action, unable to cope with Doe's intellectual clues. This emphasis on the physical is also evident in his approach to acting. Here, David Fincher describes Pitt's method of working:

biographies

colour does not affect the roles he takes

> [He] doesn't want to burn himself out ... He's an intuitive ... He's
> not one of these guys who come in with a fucking game plan; his
> whole process is all about creating a happy accident ...
>
> *Pulver, 1999, p. 2*

In *Fight Club*, he is ideally cast as Tyler Durden who personifies instinctive living. He is at his happiest when fighting and impishly destroys anything he can that is associated with capitalism and bourgeois obsessions; not least, he destroys the respectable lifestyle of his 'loser alter ego', played by Edward Norton. Pitt is not always successful: in *Meet Joe Black* (1998), he is fine as the charming and sensitive young man in the coffee shop. However, in his reincarnation as Death, Pitt fails to hit the right note. This may be because the film itself was spectacularly bad.

MORGAN FREEMAN

It is rare for an actor to become a star in her or his fifties, but Freeman's breakthrough did not come until he was aged fifty-two with his Best Actor Oscar nomination for *Driving Miss Daisy* (1989); he had already had a Best Supporting Actor nod for *Street Smart* (1987). Breakthrough though *Driving Miss Daisy* was, it seemed that Freeman was destined for supporting roles such as Ned Logan in *Unforgiven* (1992). This Clint Eastwood Western also showed how Freeman is one of the few black actors whose colour does not affect the roles he takes. In 1998 he could play the President of USA in *Deep Impact* with little sense that this was out of the ordinary (of course, there never has been a black President). While 'black' ethnicity is never far away from the characters played by Eddie Murphy in his early movies, or Samuel L. Jackson's roles, with Freeman it is all but erased. Possibly because of his age, or his trustworthy persona, Freeman never articulates black culture in the way that Jackson, in particular, does through his speech and 'attitude'.

The Shawshank Redemption (1994) saw Freeman moving towards the lead and in *Se7en* he was, at least, the equal of Pitt. He did take the lead in the *Se7en*-inspired *Kiss the Girls* (1997) and its follow-up *Along Came a Spider* (2001). Whilst he is unlikely to make the A list of stars, that elite

no threat to white hegemony

bunch who can open a movie no matter how bad it is, Freeman is a recognisable name that gives an expectation of quality, if only from his performance. Freeman's persona, however, has been dogged by his breakthrough role, as he said:

> The biggest mistake I ever made was *Driving Miss Daisy*. I became this wise, old dignified black man and it caught on so quickly.
>
> *Quoted in* Screen International, *1 September 2000*

Even when Freeman has played the bad guy, as in *Hard Rain* (1998), he is not all *that* bad and he is even allowed to get away with some of the loot. Possibly because of his age, Freeman plays characters that seem old fashioned. When he wore a leather jacket, drove a sporty car and had his hair dyed black in *Kiss the Girls*, he was less convincing than normal. *Nurse Betty* (1999) was an attempt to break away from his image, here he played a hit man on his last job. But, as in *Se7en*, he insists on doing the job properly and he never killed anyone who 'didn't have it coming to them'. The only moments of unFreemanlike behaviour is when he grabs and threatens a female bartender and when he fantasises about kissing the young (and white) Betty (Rene Zellwegger).

In *Nurse Betty*, Freeman's old-fashioned persona is contrasted by the relative wildness of his son, played by Chris Rock, who has 'attitude': a resentment of the dominance of 'white' society. Placed together, Freeman seems a representative of black men from another, more subservient era. It is obviously wrong that non-white actors should find it difficult to escape their ethnicity, but this is an example of the 'burden of representation' that lies on oppressed groups. As one of the few black actors with a high profile he becomes, by default, a representative of his race. It could be that because Freeman's persona is so inoffensive, particularly when compared to actors with 'attitude', that he offers no threat to white **hegemony**. Freeman remains thoughtful and faithful (and a great actor). The latter adjective may be reinforced by his ethnicity: if black is encoded as faithful to a white audience, then there is no threat.

KEVIN SPACEY

Stardom came two decades earlier for Spacey than Freeman. Born in 1959, 1995 was Spacey's breakthrough year. He won a Best Supporting Actor Oscar for *The Usual Suspects* and made an indelible impression to a massive audience as John Doe in *Se7en*. Like Freeman, it was likely that Spacey would be relegated to supporting roles, as he did not have the usual good looks of stars. In addition, it seemed that his casting as a villain (in the films above, *A Time to Kill*, 1996, and *A Bug's Life*: the voice of Hopper, 1998) would prevent him from achieving A list status. However, his Jack Vincennes in *L.A. Confidential* (1997), who made the transition from corrupt cop to one who fought on the right side; and complete good guy Chris Sabien in *The Negotiator* (1998), led to *American Beauty* (1999) and another Oscar, this time for Best Actor.

In both *Se7en* and *The Usual Suspects*, he played characters that were in total control of the narrative (literally so in the latter). This fits in with the cynic (his *L.A. Confidential* Jack Vincennes was as cynical as they come at the start) who believes they can see through the surface to the corruption that inevitably lies beneath, whereas others do not get the whole picture. In *American Beauty*, his Lester Burnham is a victim of circumstance at the start, he is in a mid-life crisis and – he states – 'dead already'. However, he becomes the Spacey we recognise when, after smoking dope, he takes control of his life. It could be, with *American Beauty*'s success, that Spacey will make the A list, like another not conventionally handsome actor, Tom Hanks.

director as auteur

I'm always interested in movies that *scar*.

Fincher quoted in Salisbury, 1996, p. 83

Whilst certain directors – such as Jean Renoir in France and Fritz Lang in Germany – have always been considered as artists who expressed a personal vision in their films, it was believed that Hollywood's studio system of mass production would not allow such individual expression. This assumption was broken by French film criticism in the 1950s and was taken up in the 1960s, by Andrew Sarris in America and *Movie* magazine in Britain. These critics suggested that certain directors, such as Alfred Hitchcock and Howard Hawks, could imprint their personal style on a film through their choice of script and direction, and thereby were their films' authors (**auteurs**).

Even if the studio system was a production line that left little time for experimentation and personal vision, it was an excellent training ground. Howard Hawks, for instance, had already directed twelve films before his first well-known feature, *Scarface*, appeared in 1932 and he made a total of forty-five features stretching over forty-four years. In contemporary Hollywood, directors are lucky if they get to make a film every two years; *Alien³* (1992) was David Fincher's debut feature film followed by *Se7en* three years later, *The Game* in 1997 and *Fight Club* in 1999. This makes it harder for contemporary directors to learn their craft; indeed many serve their apprenticeships in advertising and music videos.

The influx into Hollywood of directors versed in flashy mini-narratives has resulted in the glossy look of the High Concept film (see Contexts: Hollywood) exemplified by the work of Tony Scott (*Top Gun*, 1988), Ridley Scott (*Gladiator*, 2000), Adrian Lyne (*Fatal Attraction*, 1989) and Michael Bay (*Bad Boys*, 1996). David Fincher began his directorial career in the 1980s with music videos for Paula Abdul, Aerosmith ('Janie's Got Your Gun') and, probably most enduringly, Madonna's 'Express Yourself', 'Oh Father', 'Bad Girl' and 'Vogue'.

The slick surfaces of the High Concept movie are often criticised because that is all they are, surfaces with no depth. These films' requirement to look good often supersedes the need to offer meaning. This is fine for music videos and advertisements, whose primary function is marketing, but film, as an art form, can offer both entertainment and depth. This lack of meaning is symptomatic of **postmodernism**: *Gladiator*, a 'sword and sandal' epic and one of 2000's biggest hits, was accompanied throughout by Hans Zimmer's occasionally *Celtic*-sounding score. While it sounded good, it did not contribute to the *Roman* milieu.

It would be wrong to assume that High Concept movies are necessarily exercises in eye candy; they can also comment on contemporary issues.

scratching on the surface

For example, the Tony Scott-directed *Enemy of the State* (1998) critiqued the use of modern surveillance techniques.

David Fincher has found his background no impediment to either making a personal statement in his films or offering a **mise-en-scène** that rewards in-depth analysis. Even Fincher's videos are carefully constructed: 'Express Yourself' (1989) takes the look of Fritz Lang's *Metropolis* (1926) to yield an expressionist visual treat and 'Oh Father' bases itself on Orson Welles's *Citizen Kane*. Despite this, Fincher has professed not to like his music videos (Salisbury, 1996), seeing them simply as a way of learning how to use particular pieces of equipment. However, there are similarities between his films and videos.

'Judith' (2000), a video made for A Perfect Circle, reproduces the 'underground' look of the credits of *Se7en*. The scratching on the surface of the music video draws attention to itself as a *text* and eschews the usual anonymity of classical film style. Such scratching also appears in the home movie sequences of *The Game*. The title sequence of *Se7en* is constructed like a music video; it is edited to Nine Inch Nails's 'Closer'. It looks as if it is jumping in the projector and this, along with what looks like repairs made with old bits of film lead, is also modernist in the way it draws attention to itself as a film.

The work of Fritz Lang is not only evident in 'Express Yourself', mentioned above. *Se7en*, in particular, draws upon themes evident in Lang's work:

> [The] struggle with a systematic order often becomes staged as a battle to control the narrative structure of the film itself, as if the attempt of these characters to seize control of the Destiny-machine mimicked the power of the director over the film.
>
> *Gunning, 2000, p. 16*

In *Se7en*, John Doe is in control: as Somerset says at the end, 'John Doe has the upper hand'. Somerset and Mills struggle, and ultimately fail, to unpick the story being written by Doe (see Narrative and Form: Story & Plot). Doe's control of the narrative is almost equal to that of the director. Another Langian motif evident in *Se7en* is time: the film's plot covers

a subversive film maker

seven days and finishes at seven o' clock on the seventh day; Somerset goes to sleep to the sound of the metronome.

Lang's *Mabuse* trilogy (*Dr. Mabuse, the Gambler*, 1922, *The Testament of Dr. Mabuse*, 1932, and *The Thousand Eyes of Dr. Mabuse*, 1960) features the eponymous master criminal who has more than a passing similarity to John Doe:

> ... the man who prepares his crimes quasi-scientifically before executing them himself ... Dr. Mabuse, who declares, 'I am the Law', is the perfect criminal, the puppet master who organises off stage the perfect crime.
>
> *Lang quoted in Gunning, 2000, p. 96*

Lang's Hollywood films included the well-regarded serial killer movie *While the City Sleeps* (1956). In this, as in his earlier serial killer film *M* (1931), Lang emphasises how serial killing is part of mass culture. The central characters work for a newspaper company and use women in an attempt to capture the killer to further their own careers. This cynicism was slightly less evident in his gangster movie *The Big Heat* (1953), which invokes, but does not entirely endorse:

> ... the typical action hero of the 50s, the man who takes the law into his own hands, restores justice and in the process gains (or regains) a new sense of community and an ability to love ... [a] drama of reintegration and rehumanisation.
>
> *Ibid., p. 432*

This type of action hero is still evident in the twenty-first century but not in *Se7en*. The would-be action hero of this film is destroyed along with his family.

It is arguable that David Fincher makes movies as art rather than commerce and in this sense draws upon the European tradition of culture (see Contexts: Cultural Contexts). It is not stretching a point to dub him a subversive film maker, something very difficult to be within the institution of Hollywood. For example, film critic Alexander Walker, reviewing *Fight Club* (1999) in the *Evening Standard*, vilified the film:

> The movie is not only anti-capitalist but anti-society, and, indeed, anti-God.

Quoted in Pulver, 1999, p. 2

While Walker is a particularly conservative critic, Fincher seems to have the ability to raise the ire of many reviewers (see Trailer) and it is certainly no mean feat to make an anti-capitalist movie (the ending of *Fight Club* does suggest the destruction of mega-corporations would be a positive step) with the capitalist Hollywood's money. Twentieth Century Fox studio head, Bill Mechanic, lost his job in summer 2000 after a string of high profile box office flops, which included Fincher's film. That Fincher could make a $68 million *art* movie was due to *Se7en*'s $350 million worldwide gross.

Fincher's first film, *Alien³* (1992), took out much of the testosterone-horror of the first two movies and turned the renewal of the franchise into a prison movie where a shorn Ripley evoked the Joan of Arc of Carl Dreyer's 1927 classic *La Passion de Jeanne d'Arc*. As in *Se7en*, we see little violence, there are cut aways just before the victim gets it and we return to see the aftermath.

Religion is evident in Fincher's films. The religious imagery at the end of *Alien³*, where Ripley sacrifices herself, Christ-like, to save humankind by diving into the hellish inferno of the foundry, was echoed in *Se7en*'s use of the crucifix (see Narrative and Form: Characters). An establishing shot of the environment of the planet in *Alien³* shows a crucifix shape in the foreground as two suns set. In addition, the prisoners had embraced religion to atone for their sins.

The lighting of *Alien³* is similar to that of *Se7en* in that the film is 'under lit' and suffused with brown hues. Less successful was Fincher's handling of action sequences, done so brilliantly in the later film. There is never a clear sense of space in the prison camp and so when the alien suddenly appears out of nowhere, it seems as though it has done just that. The set design, following on from the first two *Alien* movies, is Gothic in character (see Contexts: Cultural Contexts). The camp seems to exist in a state of entropy: it is overwhelmed in dirt and steam flushes into virtually every location.

the profuse use of low-angle shots

Fincher has described how he found it difficult to handle studio interference when making the film, it was his debut feature and he had not yet turned thirty. Indeed, his state of mind was such that it could have also been his last feature; then the script of Se7en came along (see Contexts: Production History).

The Se7en follow-up, The Game (1997), took the paranoia that infected his first two films into the life of millionaire Nicholas van Orton (Michael Douglas). The opening sequence immediately, formally, takes us into Se7en territory with a home movie that appears to misfeed in the projector just as the credits of the earlier film seem to do. At the end of the sequence, van Orton's father disappears into the darkness.

The Game is an Oedipal drama where van Orton must free himself of his father's influence; and this is van Orton's forty-eighth birthday, the age his father killed himself. Van Orton's house has Gothic grandeur and the profuse use of low-angle shots and 'dark' lighting, give the movie a film noir edge. The plot, too, is noirish with its convoluted layers where reality and pretence merge indistinguishably. The scene where van Orton realises that Christine's house is not real has a sharp paranoid resonance; as for the central character of The Truman Show (1998), reality is not what it seems.

Van Orton's maverick brother (Sean Penn) makes it clear that the protagonist is trapped in the material expectations of his father. He buys van Orton 'the game', as a birthday present, from CRS in an attempt to wake his sibling from his bourgeois existence. CRS's offices, representing Corporate America, are filmed in such a way that they are given a metallic and inhuman edge. Their pristine look was also evident in American Psycho (2000), a serial killer movie that satirised the shallowness of 1980s' yuppies.

Van Orton is eventually reborn when he wakes up in a coffin in Mexico, the developing world. The final split with his father is made explicit when van Orton pawns the watch his father had given him, on his eighteenth birthday, to buy a bus ticket. He returns, makes a rapprochement with his ex-wife, who he had soullessly spoken to on his birthday, and then

subliminal pornographic images

completes the paranoid narrative by 'killing' his brother. Like *Fight Club*, the narrative is both playful and tight.

Fight Club is very funny and, to those who hold their lifestyle dear, disturbing. The protagonist, played by Edward Norton, sits on his toilet looking at an IKEA catalogue that, he says, is the new pornography. His room is transformed into a catalogue display. He is trapped in his materialist environment and only the anarchic (and increasingly fascist) Tyler Durden can help him escape. Unlike *Se7en*, where moral degradation was taken as read, *Fight Club* offers a political perspective where the bourgeois obsession with possessions is taken to be the villain.

Durden's house is a Gothic wreck situated in an industrial wasteland and on a number of occasions, most obviously just after the would-be vet had been threatened, the film looks like it is going to 'break out' of the projector. This trademark Fincher touch, evident in *Se7en* and *The Game*, suggests the fabric of the (bourgeois) world is about to be torn. Just as in Durden's exploits in cinemas, where he inserts subliminal pornographic images into children's film, bourgeois respectability is shockingly challenged. Indeed, Durden did the same to *Fight Club*; check out the blurred images right at the film's end.

Fincher's modernism is also evident in the occasional direct address to camera and the description of 'cigarette burns', used by projectionists so they know when a reel is about to end: Durden points to one illustrating 'Ed Norton's' voice-over.

Fight Club has claims to being the last great movie of the twentieth century; David Fincher is sure to make many of the great films of the twenty-first.

narrative & form

Narratives are designed to convey information, which may be fictional or factual. Most film narratives are fictional and self-contained so the whole story is told in one text. While television also broadcasts self-contained narratives, seriality is much more likely to feature. Serial narratives cover more than one episode, unlike series narratives, such as *Buffy, the Vampire Slayer*, which usually has one narrative each episode.

Seriality has a special fascination as, when successful, it keeps us hooked, over a long period time, to find out what will happen next. Serials will often use cliffhangers at the end of an episode in an attempt to get the audience to tune in the next time; soap operas use this device. In serial killer films, this seriality is incorporated into a self-contained text: the cliffhangers are the next murder. The investigators try and identify the killer before the next victim dies.

story & plot

Bordwell and Thompson (1993) described the Russian Formalists' way of distinguishing between story (*fabula*) and plot (*syuzhet*): the story is all the events shown *and* implied by the film in chronological order; the plot consists *only* of the events shown, which may not be chronological, plus added details such as incidental music and credits.

Everything that originates from the world created by the narrative is called the diegesis; that is, what we can see on the screen and the sounds that emanate from the space inhabited by the characters. Anything that is added to the narrative world, such as incidental music, voice-overs or titles, is non-diegetic. For instance, if music is playing within a room we can see on screen, or is obviously emanating from somewhere nearby, it is considered diegetic; however, if the music cannot be heard in room, it only exists on the soundtrack and so is non-diegetic.

the detective's task

In detective fiction, the typical story consists of: (a) crime conceived; (b) crime planned; (c) crime committed; (d) crime discovered; (e) detectives investigate; (f) detectives reveal (a), (b) and (c). The plot normally begins with the discovery of the crime or the committing of the crime (usually with the perpetrator kept anonymous). In *Se7en*, the story and plot relate to one another as follows:

STORY **PLOT**

a) Crime conceived: Doe decides to be an 'avenging angel'

b) Crime planned: Doe plans for over a year at least five of the murders

c) Crime committed: the first murder (Gluttony)

d) Crime discovered: Gluttony

e) Detectives investigate: Mills and Somerset start out on their quest

f) Detectives reveal the reasons for a, b, and c, when finding Doe's apartment; Somerset and Mills reach some understanding as to Doe's motives.

As we do not see steps (a) to (c), these form part of the story only; the plot only reveals the complete story at step (f). So the plot runs from (d) to (f); the story runs from (a) to (f). The detective's task is to piece together the story from the plot and thus solve the crime. *Se7en* subverts this by never really getting to point (f): they find Doe's residence, but not Doe; they cannot decode the masses of evidence that Doe has left; Doe gives himself up denying the detectives a triumphant end to their quest for justice.

Se7en's plot begins with Somerset preparing for work; he then attends the scene of a murder (the victim is played by Andrew Kevin Walker, the film's scriptwriter) where he meets Mills. It is likely that our expectation is that this is the first in the series of murders. Although the investigating detective tells Somerset that 'it was the wife', we would not necessarily assume this to be the case. We are familiar with narratives that show a hero looking beyond the obvious and thus finding the truth of who actually did the killing (see, for example, *Jennifer 8*, 1992).

villains are not usually given such control

Texts may be unconvincing in their *dénouement*, such as the ending of *Sliver* (1993) where the murderer is ridiculed rather than captured.

The plotting of *Se7en* is probably one of the reasons the film was so successful even though, on the face of it, is it relatively straightforward: Doe kills a series of people, is pursued without success by Mills and Somerset, and then gives himself up. However, the experience of watching the film, particularly the first time, is bewildering, especially at the moment Doe gives himself up (see below). In addition, Doe's control over events, as a master criminal, seems almost supernatural. However, the film is set in a recognisably contemporary and rational world.

As the trio go into a modern wilderness at the end, with Doe entrapped in the back of the car, we cannot imagine what trick he has in store. Narrative convention suggests something climactic is going to happen (imagine arriving at the high tension towers, Doe breaks down, regrets his actions and is then driven back to jail). Somerset has alluded to supernatural possibilities – 'If a UFO should spring from his head' – and this seems to be the only way Doe can do some more evil when he is in custody. The fact that he has prepared the perfect *dénouement*, his own death and the damnation of the hero, testifies to Doe's brilliance. He is the narrator of the film in the sense that he is in control of events. It is he who controls the plot and so writes the story. Villains are not usually given such control.

todorov & propp

Narrative is not only a linear cause-effect structure, it can also be considered as a dialectical arrangement where opposing forces come together and form a synthesis at its conclusion. Tzvetan Todorov described this as consisting of five stages:

- A statement of equilibrium: the city (see Contexts: Cultural Contexts) where murder is commonplace (shown in the film's second scene)

- disruption of the equilibrium: the discovery of the first murder uttony) everyone could be a victim

We then see Somerset prepare for bed before the credit sequence. Then, after the credits, with the day 'Monday' non-diegetically appearing on the screen, Mills, in an echo of the previous scene with Somerset, is shown preparing for work when he is called to the scene of the first murder. It is the discovery of the first murder in the series that is the narrative disruption (see below).

Serial killer narratives offer a variation to the conventional crime narrative (the a to f pattern described above) as the murders are still in progress and so the detectives have a dual task: to find out who is doing it *and* to try and pre-empt the next killing. In order to prevent another killing, the detectives need to work out the killer's *modus operandi*, and so predict where the killer will strike next. In narrative terms, the detective then manages to read the story before it becomes part of the plot. Doing this allows him to apprehend the killer. In addition, serial killer narratives strike a chord with audiences because of the very randomness of the killings. There is a sense that anyone, and everyone, could be a victim of the killer.

PLOT

Plots are not constrained by time. They can consist of numerous flashbacks, or even flash-forwards, neither of which are used in *Se7en*. The plotting of *Se7en* is tightly structured chronologically, covering seven days that are signed by titles. There are, however, many events that occur before the plot begins. Sloth, for instance, has been rotting in bed for nearly a year and Gluttony has already been tortured for a number days; these events belong only to the story.

When we consider plotting, we are looking at narrative as a ca' structure. This gives narratives credibility in the eyes of *' it does not matter what happens as long as it is r the narrative world. In science fiction, we can bel fly; in horror, monsters do exist. If, in mysteries f' offers no explanation for what is happening are likely to be disappointed. David ((1997) refuses to offer any explanation (th

22

3. A recognition of the disruption: Somerset sees that the murder is the first of a series almost immediately and thereby declines the case as this 'can't be my last'

4. An attempt to repair the disruption: the detectives attempt to apprehend the killer

5. The equilibrium is restored: the city remains a place where murder is commonplace

Disruptions usually make the narrative world a worse place. In *Se7en*, however, it is simply yet another murder. The initial situation (the equilibrium) of *Se7en* shows the world to be a hellish location and draws upon a tradition of portraying the city as a place of evil. Most narratives conclude with a 'happy ever after' feeling when the problem has been resolved; at the conclusion of *Se7en*, although the killer will no longer kill, the ending could hardly be darker as the hero is damned.

We can extend Todorov's analysis of structure to that of Vladimir Propp who focused on Russian folk tales. In Proppian terms, the disruption of the equilibrium is caused by the villain and has to be resolved by the hero. In doing so, the hero is likely to save a princess who is threatened by the villain. The terms, particularly 'princess', refer to the fairy-tale origins of Propp's analysis; the princess is any character, or group of people, who is threatened by the disruptive force (which can be human or animal or natural, such as a volcano). In this sense, narratives, particularly those that are action-based, can be seen as a battle between the hero and villain, and these often represent good and evil (see Theme: the Seven Deadly Sins). Inevitably, in order for the equilibrium to be restored, good usually triumphs. (It should be noted that Propp was referring to narrative *functions* and not characters as such.)

Propp suggested that narratives had a maximum of thirty-one functions, which fitted the same pattern as that suggested by Todorov; Propp's structure offers much more detail. Most plot time focuses on point four of Todorov's framework. This corresponds to functions sixteen to eighteen in Propp:

todorov & propp

the punishment he desires

Kevin Spacey made an indelible
impression as John Doe, the
villain who achieves the punishment
he desires

no 'happy ever after' ending

16. Hero and villain join in direct combat
17. Hero is branded
18. Villain is defeated

Direct combat between the hero and villain begins at the moment Doe returns home to find the detectives outside his door. Mills chases Doe, in one of the film's most dramatic sequences, and he is branded when Doe hits him on the head. Mills only survives because Doe – as he tells the detective later – allows him to. However, whilst many heroes are branded, and so bear the scars of battle, most succeed; Mills does not. After the branding, in conventional narratives, the hero goes on to defeat the villain. In *Se7en* this never happens and, in the scene following the detectives' investigation of Doe's apartment, the villain gives himself up.

From this point on, the Proppian narrative structure is perverted (the numbers refer to Propp's functions):

19. The villain's capture does not restore the equilibrium as there are three other deaths to be revealed: Tracy's, Doe's and, figuratively, Mills's
20. The hero does not return home
25. The hero is given a further difficult task (to take Doe to a specified location) but he fails to resist Doe's plan
27. The hero is not recognised for his deeds but is punished
30. The villain achieves the punishment he desires
31. There can be no 'happy ever after' ending or heterosexual coupling for the hero

(See Lacey, 2000, pp. 56–8 for a detailed Proppian analysis of *Se7en*.)

It becomes clear that Mills is not simply a narrative hero, he is also a princess, a 'victim hero' who needs to save himself. However, the narrative of *Se7en* is no fairy tale and in the battle between good and evil, the latter triumphs.

characters

MILLS

As noted in Background: Director as auteur, Mills is a typical man of action; even his name suggests movement. He is contrasted directly with Somerset who is, in many ways, his opposite. The film's first scene shows the meticulous Somerset preparing for work, checking his appearance in the mirror. The post-credit scene shows Mills doing the same. However, his tie is put on over his head and his appearance is shambolic. The film's poster juxtaposes Pitt and Freeman with their shadowed faces merging together: white and black; young and old; physical and mental; idealistic and cynical.

That Mills is a sacrificial figure is made clear by the **mise-en-scène** when he awaits Somerset at the scene of the Gluttony killing. Mills holds two cups of coffee and his posture is hunched against the driving rain; behind him is a telegraph pole in the shape of a cross. This is echoed in the final scene when he shoots Doe: a cross-like pylon stands between Mills and Somerset. Mills's eventual obliteration is foreshadowed in the earlier scene when he is suddenly blocked from our view by, it transpires, Somerset opening the boot of his car. The soundtrack reinforces the sinister resonance of this with a weird violin sound.

Mills's subordinate position is also emphasised in this scene by his movement toward Somerset, who refuses the proffered coffee, and in the way he then follows the older man into the building. The initially combative relationship between the two characters is also made evident by the mise-en-scène when they first meet (see Style: Mise-en-scène). However Mills's wife brings them together (see below) and, in a key sequence, Mills and Somerset discuss the case in a bar after they had interrogated witnesses to the Lust killing; previously Mills had refused Somerset's invite to a bar. It becomes clear in the conversation that Somerset had once been like Mills, but had his youthful innocence drained from him by being in the city too long (he says 'you cannot afford to be this naïve'). Later, as they shave their chests for 'wiring' before they take Doe on the final journey, Somerset says he wants Mills to be ready for anything. Mills's response, which in the past had been dismissive of his partner's fatherly concern, is a simple: 'I will'. He has accepted Somerset's superiority and a father-son relationship has developed between them. However, when Mills starts a question, 'You know ...?', although prompted to finish by Somerset, he walks away. Despite their closeness, the men still find if difficult to communicate.

While Mills talks constantly, Somerset prefers silence. This was in part motivated by Freeman's acting style, his preference for using facial expression over words, which led to his dialogue being cut. Pitt's dialogue, on the other hand, was increased (Dyer, 1999, p. 51).

Although Mills is Somerset's inferior throughout, Se7en does not simply state that action per se is bound to fail. After Mills bashes Doe's door down, to Somerset's incredulity, the latter then looks on with a certain amount of admiration as Mills bribes a drug addict to tell a cop she had called them to 'legitimise' his action. And Mills's idealism shines against Somerset's cynicism; he may even have convinced the retiring cop to stay on. When he suggests that Somerset only says the world is a terrible place as an excuse to quit, his partner does not contradict him.

Mills, though, is shown to be out of his depth in this city. He is given the Gould case and has to endure cops whispering about his rookie status as he enters Gould's office. At the same time, he sees on television the District Attorney state that the force has its 'best men on the job'.

Ultimately his desire for action, for physical rather than intellectual labour, proves his undoing. His attack on Doe disguised as a photographer prefigures his tragic decision to kill at the end. Somerset looks on in bewilderment and says, 'we have to divorce ourselves from our emotions'. Mills cannot even control his anger at being unable to understand 'fucking Dante' and 'faggot poetry' and he bashes the books on his car's dashboard. Mills's proletarian sensibility is also demonstrated in his beer drinking in contrast to Somerset's preference for wine. Mills pours wine into a beer glass and when Somerset notices it, his expression is one of mingled surprise and horror.

Mills is a sympathetic character not simply because he is played by Brad Pitt, but because he wants to be a champion, he wants to do good and save people. In Se7en's view of the modern world, this is not possible.

trapped in his environment

SOMERSET

Somerset is the intellectual: he intuitively knows that the Gluttony murder is the first of a series and he understands Doe's references, or at least knows where to research them. As a detective, he belongs to the nineteenth century where Poe's Augustin Dupin and Conan Doyle's Sherlock Holmes locked wits, rather than brawn, with their adversaries. He only comes close to anger twice, when Mills breaks down the door to Doe's apartment and when Doe goads his partner at the end; on both occasions he is able to control his passion.

However, he also appears trapped in his environment, hence his desire to escape to somewhere 'a long way from here'. He is in the twilight of his career, as his name suggests (sunset). In the opening scene, the wide-angle lens foreshortens the scene's depth of field, making his apartment seem even more enclosed than it is. Vertical edges cut into the frame on either side, reducing the lateral space of the widescreen. Somerset is even cut through by the left-hand edge. As he moves toward the camera a chess set, in the foreground, comes into focus; it is an emblem of Somerset's penchant for intellectual challenge. He listens to jazz (Charlie Parker's 'Now's the Time') as a mark of his ethnicity (jazz as 'black' music) and his cultural appreciation.

His entrapment is further emphasised by the soundtrack: in the first scene we can hear perennial traffic noises (including police sirens), neighbours' voices and television sets. After he has met Mills, we return to Somerset's place, this time the neighbours' voices have taken on an expressionist quality as they echo unrealistically. It is as if they are voices in his head and the extraneous noises of city life have penetrated his mind so much that he can only sleep to the accompaniment of the monotonous sound of a metronome. However, as the case reaches its climax, even this comfort is denied him and he smashes the time marker.

Somerset is old fashioned both in the clothes he wears, which come out of a 1940s' film noir (see Contexts: Genre), and in his gentlemanly manners toward Tracy. When she invites him to dinner, he demurs but after being persuaded, he graciously states: 'In that case I'll be delighted'.

characters

He has dedicated himself to his job, so much so that his captain says he was born to do it. He persuaded his partner to abort their child because of his bleak view of the world and so is left alone both regretting his decision and knowing it was the right one.

Somerset is given the valedictory pronouncement and promises he will be around, a studio-inspired ending that offers the only ray of hope in the film: he says he agrees with the final part of Ernest Hemingway's statement that 'the world is a fine place and worth fighting for'.

DOE

John Doe is the name given to men who refuse to identify themselves. As such it is a perfect name for a serial killer who revels in anonymity (see Contexts: Cultural Contexts). All that is ever found out about Doe is that he is 'independently wealthy'. However, unlike other serial killers, such as *M*'s Franz Becker and *Blue Steel*'s (1990) Eugene Hunt, Doe does not 'feed off his emotions'. He is not driven to kill by 'animal lust' but by intellectual hubris. In this he is like Thomas Harris's Hannibal Lecter:

> ... both Lector and Doe have the urbanity and aristocratic style of the gothic villain ...
>
> *Withall, 1996, p. 63b*

This results in a fascistic attitude that justifies murder by dehumanising people that are defined as inferior to oneself. In addition to this, however, Doe wishes to corrupt the innocent. In this he is a Faustian character who usurps:

> ... the prerogative of the deity to judge and punish.
>
> *Ibid., p. 63a*

Doe's view of the world is similar to Somerset's and they are both intellectuals. However, while one tries to solve crimes to bring the malfeasant to justice, the other acts as a vigilante. Doe is undoubtedly psychotic but in his conversation with Mills, in the car, he draws comparisons between himself and the young detective. He suggests that

a visual sign of her imprisonment

the only difference between them, morally, is due to consequences, otherwise Mills would be happy to beat Doe to a pulp in contravention of the law.

TRACY

Tracy is a problematic character from the point of view of gender. Arguably she is in the film simply to act as a victim. Women are secondary characters in the film: either victims of Doe (Lust and Pride) or married to a victim (Greed). Tracy hates the city, she is only there because of her husband, clearly cannot cope with the environment and needs *male* advice on her pregnancy. Her husband even apologises for swearing in front of her. She is shown looking at her husband watching sport from behind wooden struts that are a visual sign of her imprisonment. She awakes, after the supper party, to find the men gone on their mission.

However, she is a positive influence on Mills and Somerset and brings them together; that this is explicitly to do with gender is evident when Tracy greets their arrival for supper with, 'Hello men'. She then goes on to embarrass her husband by introducing the detectives to one another by their first names. Men are represented as both unfriendly and repressed individuals.

theme: the seven deadly sins

The Seven Deadly Sins were so described as they were deemed to be morally wrong and would lead to other sins. St Thomas Aquinas, in his *Summa Theologica*, classically described the Sins in the thirteenth century; death was the 'wages of these sins'. The Sins are a Christian, and Catholic, formulation.

As far as Catholicism was concerned, over-eating, greed, laziness, sexual intercourse, pride, envy and anger were evil. From a contemporary point of view, over-eating, greed and envy are often characterised as wrong but it would depend upon what type of pride was felt as to whether this would be considered negatively. Laziness is not seen to be good; however, in an era where many people work extremely long hours, it may have its virtues. Anger is often celebrated as being passionate about something and can regularly be seen displayed on talk shows (like Jerry Springer's) as an expression of 'wound culture' (see Contexts: Cultural Contexts). In western society, sex is usually represented as something to be desired.

As we have seen, Doe represents evil. We can assume then that Doe's reasons for acting are also evil. In this, *Se7en* is commenting upon contemporary society. These comments, however, are anything but straightforward. Some of Doe's arguments are reasonable (greed is wrong), but others betray his reactionary stance (lust is wrong). This lack of coherence could be seen to be either inconsistency on the part of the film or as a reflection of the ideologically-confused state of western society:

GLUTTONY

In contemporary western society, slimness, for women at least, is seen as a prerequisite for beauty. Therefore people who are not slim are deemed to be unattractive, though there are obviously degrees of fatness. By contemporary standards, the ideal beauty is a scrawny super model, many of whom are under-weight. So even women who are the 'correct' weight may feel 'fat'. At the other end of the scale are obese individuals whose weight is unhealthy. In between these extremes are people who may be overweight for their height (according to official statistics), but this suits their lifestyle.

It is arguable that the modern emphasis on the ideal body is an example of 'body fascism'. If you do not conform to the ideal, then you are in some way inferior. Keep fit, along with healthy eating, has become very popular in the west during the last thirty years; the advertising images of such routines as Body Pump even looks fascist, with groups of people moving together with an intent and solemn expression.

a flawed legal process

The Gluttony victim is clearly obese and certainly looks unattractive, particularly as a cadaver. Few, however, would follow Doe's logic that he therefore deserved to die.

GREED

Though greed may have been deemed good during the excesses of the 1980s – and only by those who were benefiting from the unequal distribution of wealth – today's corporate 'fat cats' are regularly vilified in the press, though this does not diminish their appetite. There is also a consensus that the more money one has the better, no matter what the cost to others or to the environment. Arguably the west is greedy, feeding off the developing world.

If the lawyer Gould's riches have been gained through greed, it must be assumed that he knew he was doing wrong when defending guilty people. However, the legal system demands this. In addition, it seems clear that the more money one has to spend on a lawyer then the greater the likelihood of acquittal. There are a disproportionate amount of poor, black Americans on death row because of their lack of funds. It should also be noted that there is little evidence that the Sloth victim could afford Gould's services.

Doe's murder of the lawyer draws upon a common theme in cop movies where the legal apparatus is shown to be failing. As a result, the police see criminals freed who they know to be guilty. This is the theme of the *Dirty Harry* series (1971–83) where Harry is played by Clint Eastwood. By stepping outside the framework of the law, Harry becomes a vigilante, an individual who takes the law into his own hands.

It may be true that guilty people are found innocent through a flawed legal process, but what the vigilante movies fail to consider is the reason why people are assumed innocent until found guilty. The possibilities of miscarriages of justice are far greater if individuals take the law into their own hands than if the due processes of law are followed. In *Se7en*, unlike vigilante movies, we are not invited to take the vigilante's side and so the murder of Gould is wrong and therefore Greed is not characterised as a sin by the film.

theme

SLOTH

Victor, the 'drug-dealing pederast' (he had sex with children), is a modern bogeyman. His death is the worst of the seven in that it takes over a year to happen. The doctor states that Sloth has suffered more pain than anyone he has encountered and that the victim still had Hell to look forward to. The scene where Sloth is found tethered to the bed is the most viscerally horrific in the film. Few would feel any sorrow for Sloth, but the horror experienced by most of the audience when he 'comes back to life' suggests some sympathy with what he has experienced. If we did not feel horror, then we would believe that Victor deserved his fate. So despite the extreme nature of Sloth's sins, it is Doe's actions that are shown to be more evil.

LUST

Doe possesses the reactionary view of female sexuality and he describes his Lust victim as the 'disease-spreading whore'. He not only punishes the prostitute, the 'john' also suffers as he is forced to do the actual murder. One of the scene's most chilling scenes is the interrogation of the 'john' (brilliantly played by Leland Orser) when he describes what he is forced to do.

Conventional morality is rather confused about sex: on the one hand, the traditionalists would like to see it confined to marriage, whilst popular culture, as expressed in the media, celebrates certain forms of sexuality with brazen abundance. Lust can be destructive, it may lead to rape, but it is also natural. Anyone who is disgusted with lust aligns themselves, in terms of the film, with John Doe.

PRIDE

Pride is linked to the Gluttony murder as it is also to do with appearance. Another facet of the body fascism, alluded to above, is the growth of cosmetic surgery. While this can be obviously beneficial to render any extreme disfigurement innocuous, the growth of breast enlargement, for example, suggests an unhealthy obsession with what the perfect body is deemed to be.

This murder, like Mills's destruction, is self-inflicted and so proves Doe's point that anyone bound up with their own appearance would prefer to die rather than be seen as ugly. Pride, though, has wider resonance than this: pride in one's work is surely not a sin.

ENVY

Doe's sin is his desire to live a normal life like Mills. This does not quite ring true as Doe holds his fellow, normal human beings in contempt; his notebook tells the story of how he vomited over a man who engaged him in casual conversation. Presumably the only sin that Doe could commit would be pride in his work, or possibly wrath. To object to this inconsistency would be unfair on the scriptwriter as, overall, the narrative is beautifully constructed. In addition, as envy is *Doe's* sin, Tracy is an innocent victim even in Doe's terms. Doe sins in killing her.

WRATH

This sin runs throughout Mills's character (see above) and is one half of the film's crucial opposition: emotion versus intellect. Allowing anger to determine ones actions leads to terrible consequences, which is graphically dramatised by *Se7en*'s climactic scene as Mills realises the truth of what Doe has said to him.

This is a brilliant climax as the audience is positioned to share Mills's viewpoint. What Doe has done to Tracy is as evil as his other murders, but this time the person emotionally closest to the victim can act as jury, judge and executioner. On one level, Doe deserves to die; he is evil incarnate. Believers in capital punishment have a cast iron case with this man. However, the film suggests otherwise: to kill Doe is as much a sin as those that Doe has committed. This view is clear in Somerset's response, though he, too, is momentarily sucked into anger when he slaps Doe to quiet the villain's goading.

It is the almost subliminal flash of Tracy's face that decides Mills's actions and we can understand why he kills. How many in the audience would not do so in the same circumstances? However, to do so makes us the same as Doe, in other words 'ordinary' people can be as evil as Doe. Ultimately, the film suggests, it is part of the human condition to be evil.

style

mise-en-scène

Mise-en-scène refers to what is 'in the picture'. At a level of denotation, this would simply be a description of objects within the frame and the camera's position in relation to them. For example, as Mills and Somerset leave the scene of the murder before the credit sequence, the camera tracks their movement while they have a discussion. In the hands of many directors (dubbed *metteur en scenes* by French critics who first identified **auteurs**: see Background: Director as auteur), the camera would be positioned in order to best facilitate an understanding of what is being said, how it is being said (the acting) and the setting. However, the best directors will do all of the above and add the camera itself to the equation.

As noted in our discussion of David Fincher in Background, contemporary directors get little opportunity to make films and so it is difficult to learn an immensely complex craft. Fincher, however, is in the mould of directors who use the camera position to add to the elements within the mise-en-scène. For example, in the scene mentioned above, the camera tracks, from a low angle, Mills's and Somerset's movement down the sidewalk. The low angle exaggerates the position the characters are in relation to one another as first one, and then the other, is accorded a dominant position in the frame. This **blocking** occurs in five phases:

1. As they leave the building, Mills is positioned higher in the frame when he refuses Somerset's invite to have a drink in a bar

2. As they walk, from right to left, the camera tracks their movements and Somerset asks Mills why he has come to the city ('Why here?'). Somerset is now higher in the frame; Mills is knocked back by a passer by, thus keeping him behind and below Somerset

3. When Mills answers the question ('Same reasons as you, I guess'), he has caught up and the characters are equals in the frame. They have stopped walking

4. Somerset moves towards the camera and repeats his question: he is once again dominant

5. Mills then steps towards the camera, putting him above Somerset again, and states he 'thought he could do some good'

6. Somerset then moves forward, and the characters are on an equal footing. At this point, Mills agrees that Somerset is in charge

From the point of view of script, it is clear that the characters are feeling each other out. Fincher's use of the low-angle tracking shot, which would have been conventionally filmed at eye level, creates a much more dynamic mise-en-scène as the discussion becomes a *visual*, as well as verbal, duel for superiority. Each vies for control and though Somerset has the last word, Mills's position in the mise-en-scène is as an equal at the end of the scene.

The low-angle shot is characteristic of film noir (see Contexts: Genre) and the Expressionist cinema from which film noir derived. Expressionism is characterised by a very exaggerated, and unbalanced, mise-en-scène that often reflects the mental state of characters. Fritz Lang was one of the great Expressionist film makers in Germany during the 1920s (see Background: Director as auteur).

Establishing shots in *Se7en* are invariably unbalanced. Fincher often uses a wide-angle lens and a low-angle shot of the exterior of buildings. However, ignoring the rule of thirds, which suggest one third of the frame would be occupied by the sky, the claustrophobia of the city is emphasised by showing little or no sky at all.

set design and setting

In Narrative and Form: Character, comment was made on Somerset's apartment; while Mills's apartment is a brighter place, perennial interruptions, courtesy of subway trains, rattle their abode. As in Somerset's home, the sounds of the city penetrate the domestic space;

there is no escape. The most important setting in the film is the city. It seeps into everything, even the countryside in the film's climactic ending (see Contexts: Cultural Contexts). Possibly only the Gothic grandeur of the library, which emphasises its solidity and gives it the authority to dispense the knowledge that it has held for many years, escapes the insidious city.

The desert scenery of the final scene is ruptured by the field of high tension towers, presumably supplying power to the city. This dramatic landscape is introduced by a **point of view shot** from the helicopter tracking the car: the towers suddenly appear over a ridge and then, in an extreme long shot, with a massively foreshortened depth of field, the car is seen trapped between a morass of pylon. The modern world has penetrated even the desert and encloses Mills, the 'victim hero'.

Doe's apartment is a perverted space hidden behind the door in an ordinary apartment block. During the chase we had seen ordinary families sharing the block with Doe but, where there was light in most apartments, in Doe's space there is darkness. Amongst the detail picked out by the camera in Doe's home is the multitude of locks on the door. Presumably Doe wants to keep the city out, though it is doubtful if many would wish to go into such a room. The place is full of handwritten books that painstakingly detail Doe's thoughts; a tool kit; empty drug containers (used on Sloth) and photographs of his victims, including Mills. Although the detectives are seeking clues, they find none. This man's way of thinking is alien to the norm. As was the case in Lila Crane's search of Norman Bates's bedroom in *Psycho*, nothing is revealed.

lighting

A crucial element of mise-en-scène is the lighting and this is used particularly expressively in *Se7en*. *Se7en* is, literally, one of the darkest movies ever made:

> The print was processed through silver retention, a seldom-used method whereby the silver that's leeched (*sic*) out during the

lighting

shot in a sepia tint

> conventional processing is rebonded. Silver retention produced
> more luminosity in the light tones and more density in the darks.
>
> *Taubin, 1996, p. 24*

Se7en is a film noir that, as the name suggests, is characterised
by blackness (see Contexts: Genre). The darkness helps convey
the bleak vision of these films. The lighting helps create the
claustrophobic space of Somerset's apartment and so emphasises his
entrapment; the lights either side of his bed seem only to cast beams a
very short distance. In the library that Somerset visits, the tables are lit
by individual green lights, suggesting decay, that add to the stygian
gloom of the place. It is worth noting, as an example of Fincher's
attention to detail, that the transition (a **dissolve**) from this scene to the
next, in a street, is made smoother by the fact that a green light is
replaced by a green leaflet, held by a passer by, in the same position in
the frame.

The cinematography of *Se7en* leaches out all but the brown tones,
making it seem as if the film was shot in a sepia tint. This monochromatic
quality harks back to black and white film noir. Other directors have used
brighter colours in their films noir: for example Martin Scorsese
emphasises red in *Taxi Driver* (1976) and Kathryn Bigelow blue in *Blue
Steel* (1990).

the shot: seeing

Seeing is crucial to detective fiction: the protagonist must read ('see') the
story from in the plot (see Narrative and Form: Story & Plot). This looking
is made explicit in *Se7en* with an emphasis on seeing as a thematic
device and through the use of point of view shots.

Doe believes that the sickness of the modern world is encapsulated in
people's inability to see the corruption that surrounds them. He berates
Mills for calling his victims innocent; only in a world 'this shitty', he
believes, could such a description be given to the deceased. Somerset has
some sympathy with this view; he describes how a man gratuitously had
his eyes gouged out.

playing with ignorance of culture

The darkness of the Gluttony murder scene obscures, at first, the fact of murder. Mills assumes it is a coronary until Somerset, who takes nothing for granted and so looks carefully, points out the corpse's feet are bound. The scene closes with the doctor pulling the dead man's face out of the bowl of spaghetti to give the audience a glance (we want no more) of his horrific visage.

As the detectives drive away from the scene, Mills questions Somerset's treatment of him (he had been sent away from the crime scene); the rain is so intense that it is barely possible to see out of the window and Mills does not understand Somerset's meticulous way of working.

When researching literature in the library, a point of view shot shows Somerset's vision coming into focus after he puts on his glasses: spectacles are associated with intellect and help the wearer to see. The object that comes into focus is Dante Alighieri's *Divine Comedy*; this text, amongst others, will offer clues to Doe's motives. Similarly, Chaucer's *The Canterbury Tales* goes out of focus as it is taken off the shelf.

Somerset's glasses also feature when he realises that Doe is preaching a sermon. In Mills's apartment we see pictures of Gould reflected in his spectacles at the moment of realisation. The photograph of Gould's wife, with blood-ringed eyes, leads them back to Gould's office which, in turn, leads them to Victor, the Sloth victim.

They need to interview Gould's wife because they do not recognise that the painting was hung upside down. Doe is playing with ignorance of culture; most people cannot tell whether abstract art is hung correctly. However, given Doe's reactionary values, it is unlikely that he would prize modern art.

music

We have already noted how jazz is used to signify Somerset's sophistication; we shall see (in Contexts: Ideology) how music is also used to mobilise ethnic considerations. In addition to this, two other types of music stand out: the title and credit sequences (Nine Inch Nails's 'Closer' and David Bowie's 'The Hearts (*sic*) Filthy Lesson') and Bach's 'Air on a G String' from Orchestral Suite number three.

music

the film does not appear to be running smoothly

Nine Inch Nails are a Goth band (see Contexts: Cultural Contexts) apparently obsessed with the mass murderer Charles Manson. A version of 'Closer' used in the title sequence, which ends with the lyrics 'take me closer to God', is a mix of music and noise. It expresses the deranged mind of Doe as we see his preparations, including cutting off his fingerprints with a razor, for his grand design. The noise aspect is complemented by the fact the film does not appear to be running smoothly through the projector, it jumps (or at least the titles do) and looks to be patched together by different bits.

David Bowie's 'The Hearts Filthy Lesson' is taken from '1. Outside: The Nathan Adler Diaries – a hyper cycle' album. Nathan Adler is a detective and, as Dyer points out, refers to Alfred Adler, a psychoanalyst who described the 'violence of the human psyche' (Dyer, 1999, p. 53).

The scene where Somerset researches the Seven Deadly Sins is particularly interesting in terms of its mix of diegetic and non-diegetic sound. Diegetic sound originates in the narrative world and so does Bach's 'Air' when it is turned on by a security guard. However, although there are a series of dissolves, suggesting passing time, as Somerset searches the library the music continues in an uninterrupted flow. It therefore becomes non-diegetic, as it originates on the soundtrack. This is particularly evident with the cross cutting between Somerset and Mills who is conducting his own research by studying the photographs of the victims. This non-diegetic soundtrack brings the characters together; after all, they have a common goal in trying to unlock the mystery of the serial killer's motivation. Indeed, the cutting is disorientating when the overhead shot of Mills momentarily appears to be of Somerset (see Editing below).

See Contexts: Cultural Contexts for a discussion of how Bach's music represents European culture. This cross cutting between the characters is also evident when they investigate Doe's apartment and helps to 'twin' the characters.

editing

Richard Dyer shows how the editing pattern, of the final journey in the car, brings together Mills and Doe:

> The cuts between Mills and Doe usually show both of them behind bars, suggesting a connection between them, that is both an anticipation of the denouement (both will be destroyed for their sin) and an implication of their similarity.
>
> *Dyer, 1999, p. 26*

Earlier in the film, the similarity between Mills and Somerset was suggested by the editing. As noted above, whilst Somerset researches the Seven Deadly Sins in the library, Mills reads reports and looks at images of the first two murders. While the non-diegetic use of Bach's 'Air' draws together the characters, the editing makes the link even more explicit.

A point of view of shot, from Mills, shows a photograph of Gluttony's bound feet. This cuts to a shot of Somerset's feet walking towards the camera. The camera moves up as it **dollies** back but stops at the books that Somerset is carrying: we are seeing him from a low-angle shot (suggesting heroism) but the focus is on the books (knowledge) of which Mills is ignorant.

An **eyeline match** follows a close up of Mills's eyes and we can read what he is seeing. Although Mills is studying the evidence, he is not seeing what Doe is doing. A cut to Somerset, continuing from a low angle, shows him reading. The editing in the next part of the sequence emphasises how the knowledge Somerset is gaining will help him understand the crimes he is investigating.

A dissolve to point of view shot of the book momentarily juxtaposes Somerset (who can still be seen) with the text he is reading: the knowledge belongs to him. Later, Mills bashes a book of *The Inferno* on the dashboard in fury: the knowledge is not his. With Somerset still superimposed upon the text (the dissolve is not complete), he turns the page, which acts as a **wipe** to the next shot, a Gustave Dore illustration of *The Inferno*. Another dissolve takes us back to Somerset but this time the camera, from its low angle, starts moving in to signify Somerset's one is psychotic

understanding. Another 'turning page' wipe returns us to Dore's images; a cut back to Somerset follows with the camera continuing its movement toward him. Another cut takes us back to the book with a **montage** of three horrific images and this is followed by a point of view shot of Somerset writing his notes. This is followed by a cut to an overhead shot, and slightly behind, of a character stretching; you think this is Somerset but it transpires it is Mills.

This sequence shows the characters together, in time if not in space, and sharing a quest for knowledge. However, only the educated one makes progress.

Mills and Somerset are similar (see also Narrative and Form: Characters), as are Mills and Doe, so then it follows that Doe and Somerset are linked. One is psychotic, the other humane, but their view of the modern world is the same.

contexts

ideology: ethnicity

Possibly because *Se7en* does not identify the city of its setting (see Cultural Contexts: The City), the film does not seem to be particularly about the mid-1990s when it was made. In addition, Somerset's clothing is straight out of a 1940s' film noir (see Genre) which helps give a timeless quality to the film. It may even be slightly old-fashioned in its representation of the city as a place of decay and moral turpitude; New York, for example, had cleaned up its act in the 1990s. Hell's Kitchen, for instance, an area of gang warfare and violence, as shown in *Sleepers* (1996) and *Bringing Out the Dead* (Martin Scorsese, 1999), is no longer the surreal place portrayed in Scorsese's film.

It was noted, in Background: Key players' biographies, that Freeman can play characters shorn of their ethnicity and this is evident on the surface of *Se7en*. The fact that Somerset is black is never raised. Although it seems to ignore the issue of race, the ethnicity of the Mills-Somerset pairing is relevant. As Richard Dyer points out, the virtual suppression of race serves to highlight that serial killing is a 'white thing':

> In this context, the Somerset-Mills duo becomes even more resonant (or counter-resonant) of ... films which explicitly pit the education, intelligence and good sense of the black investigator against whites who are both stupid and racist.
>
> *Dyer, 1999, p. 40*

Whilst Mills is certainly not portrayed as being racist or stupid (though he lacks an education in literature), Somerset's superiority as a detective is evident. That black issues do lurk in the film is further emphasised by the casting of Richard Roundtree as the DA; Roundtree played the iconic cop, Shaft, in the blaxsploitation movie of that name in 1971. In addition,

a progressive text

Marvin Gaye's 'Trouble Man' is played in the Mills's apartment; it was the title track of another 'black' movie of the early 1970s. Dyer traces the link further: the Nine Inch Nails's track, 'Closer', that runs on the credits, was recorded in mass murderer Charles Manson's house. Manson, and his 'family', believed black people should be exterminated. Also, the silver retention process used in developing the film allows the face tones of black characters to be seen clearly. This is unusual:

> There is something like a 15–20 per cent difference in the degree of light reflected by the darkest and fairest skins. It's something that has to be borne in mind when shooting people of different colours. White people need less exposure time, less light, less tightly grained stock than do black people ... Get everything right for the whites and the black faces look like blobs; get it right for the blacks, and the white faces are all bleached out.
>
> *Dyer, 1997, p. 13*

When films pair black and white characters, the white face is taken for the norm so making the black face appear undifferentiated (aiding the racist's cry, 'they all look alike'); for an example, see Sean Connery and Wesley Snipes in *Rising Sun* (1993).

The opposition of 'Somerset's mind' and 'Mills's physicality' (his desire for action) reverses the mode of representation that defines subordinate groups – in this case blacks – as being 'projected as body rather than mind' (Shohat and Stam, 1994, p. 138). In this it can be seen as a progressive text, though in other areas (see Critical Responses) it is reactionary.

cultural contexts

EUROPE AND NORTH AMERICA

The fact that we usually consider the culture of North America in relation to that of Europe is not a historical accident. European culture has had such an immense influence upon North America that other cultures are often forgotten or ignored. Not least amongst these is the culture of the native North Americans.

as trashy as fast food

It has been estimated that there were eight million Arawaks living in the Caribbean when Columbus 'discovered' the continent in 1492:

> ... within one century of the Spanish arrival, the peaceful Arawak and most of their neighbors became extinct, victims of European disease, maltreatment, and cultural upheaval.
>
> *Carroll and Noble, 1977, p. 22*

By the twentieth century, little was left of indigenous American culture and the New World had become the richest and most powerful nation on the planet. The North American continent was seen as a virgin land (hence the name of the state of Virginia), ripe for European settlement. The relationship between America and the Old World ruptured in the Revolution and Independence was declared in 1776. America was a schizophrenic nation: new (in a European sense), and the world's only truly democratic nation, but at the same time conscious of its own lack of cultural identity. Like an errant child, the New World wished to assert its identity against its European parentage. However, as much of America – the East coast in particular – was suffused with European culture, this was a difficult task.

Nineteenth-century American literature can be characterised as the search for the Great American Novel, a novel that would bear comparison with the European canon and at the same time be essentially American. This Holy Grail was attained with *Moby Dick*, by Herman Melville, published in 1851. It is now regarded as probably the greatest novel of that century, though critical incomprehension greeted it at the time it was published.

In the twentieth century, America seemed to find its cultural voice, primarily in cinema and popular music. This emphasis on entertainment rather than 'art' leads many to consider American culture to be as trashy as fast food. This viewpoint ignores the fact that cultural artefacts produced for profit can be as artistic as those produced as art. However, there does seem to remain a cultural insecurity in America. Many British actors are cast as villains (Brian Cox and Anthony Hopkins both played Hannibal Lecter); the representation of British colonials in *The Patriot*

the best at everything

(2000) was diabolical (likening the British to Nazis); the capture of the Enigma code machine, shown in *U-571* (2000), becomes, in Hollywood, an American success whereas it was a British operation; similarly, you will look in vain to find anything other than American troops in the D-Day landings of *Saving Private Ryan* (1998). It is almost as if Americans do not want to see negative representations of themselves and need to believe that they are the best at *everything*.

To assume Hollywood's entertainment is a straightforwardly American product, however, is to ignore the enormous influence Europeans have had on American cinema. As we shall see in Genre, émigré directors, such as Fritz Lang and Billy Wilder, had an immense influence on the development of film noir. In the 1990s, directors such as Wolfgang Petersen, Roland Emmerich and Paul Verhoeven have been responsible for a number of blockbuster movies.

Despite this, European culture is still seen as having more aesthetic value, financial value being the preoccupation of Hollywood. David Fincher is, however, a relatively non-commercial film maker and draws upon a European tradition in his films (see Background: Director as auteur). The clash between European and American culture is seen most interestingly, in *Se7en*, when Somerset is researching the Seven Deadly Sins.

Richard Dyer points out that much of the soundtrack of *Se7en* is a cacophonic symphony composed by the city except when a security guard puts on Bach's 'Air on a G string':

> The calm and rationality of Bach embrace ... both [Somerset and Mills], an oasis of literally and metaphorically uncontaminated sound.

> Dyer, 1999, p. 57

This scene is analysed in Style: Music, and serves to draw the characters together. However, it also draws attention to European culture: some regard Bach as the greatest composer in the western tradition and Somerset is researching great European literature, Dante and Chaucer. There are **point of view shots** (see also Style: The Shot: Seeing) of

cultural contexts

Somerset looking at Gustave Dore's horrific images illustrating *The Inferno*. This is cross cut with Mills looking at photographs of Doe's victims (he cannot look beyond the crime scene in his quest for clues) and brings together old and new images of violence. This suggests that the world has always been a violent place and contradicts Somerset's view that the modern world is particularly bad. In this, the Old World, of European tradition, is shown to be as awful as the New World of American violence. The juxtaposition of violent images with the serenity of Bach's 'Air' suggests the extremes to which humanity can go; like the concentration camp guards who read Goethe. On the one hand we have the beauty of Bach, on the other the horror of Hell (which, for the non-religious, is a metaphorical human creation).

Doe's victims look like images from the photography of Joel-Peter Witkin, a controversial artist because he uses the body parts of corpses as his subject:

> The freakier the better. A deformed foetus is nailed to a cross, a headless man is arranged on a chair, a head is split and its two halves rejoined in a kiss.
>
> *Franks, 1999, p. 34*

In Witkin's photographs, death poses for art and *Se7en*'s reference to this draws attention to Doe as a performance artist. Doe, through his meticulous planning, is performing his masterpiece: 'Seven murders in the style of the Seven Deadly Sins'. In the shop, Wild Bill mentions this as he assumed the razor-edged dildo he had created was for a performance artist. The reference is partly a sick joke but is also a comment upon performance art as being something of a joke; not real art. The use of Witkin is therefore also called into doubt: is his aesthetic used to draw attention to the sick elements of his art, so he is no 'better' than Doe, or is it used because Witkin shows 'life as it is'?

Fincher has stated he likes to make 'movies that scar', which implies he shares something of Witkin's way of representing the world. The 'poses' of the dead in *Se7en* are not simply designed to shock and so Fincher can hardly be called exploitative in his use of horror, as it is relatively

cultural contexts

restrained. We see nothing of the Lust murder and the Pride victim's face is left unseen. Compared to the *Se7en* rip-off *Resurrection* (1999), which revels in grotesque imagery, Fincher's movie leaves something to the imagination and so is far more terrifying. In referencing Witkin, he shows the grotesque and references a modern aesthetic that suggests the world is a rather sick place.

Although Fincher draws upon the European tradition, and his cinematographer Darius Khondji is French, the film remains distinctly American with its use of Hollywood stars and its relatively large budget. American culture has become, from the perspective of Europe at least, a more commercial version of the western tradition. However, it is possible that American culture will not always by reliant upon Europe. In recent years, Hispanic culture has started to make an impact; not least in Hollywood with the growing profile of such stars as Jennifer Lopez, Salma Hayek and Penelope Cruz.

GOTHIC

The Gothic is a European tradition that *Se7en*, like Witkin, draws upon. The Gothic thrived in Europe in the last third of the eighteenth century and was a reaction against industrialisation and urbanisation:

> It is a complex form situated on the edges of bourgeois culture, functioning in a dialogical relation to that culture.
>
> *Jackson, 1981, p. 96*

The Gothic deals with extremities and is often present in horror films where the monster represents the return of the Other. The Other is a psychoanalytical construction and stands for everything that a civilised society has repressed. During the Enlightenment, a period of immense scientific advance in the eighteenth century, its opposite – Unreason – was repressed:

> Unreason, silenced throughout the Enlightenment period, erupts in the fantastic art of Sade, Goya and horror fiction.
>
> *Ibid., p. 95*

cultural contexts

North America has its own form of Gothic developed in response to its New World status:

> American gothic literature criticizes America's national myth of new-world innocence by voicing the cultural contradictions that undermine the nation's claim to purity and equality.
>
> *Goddu, 1997, p. 10*

The haunting Other of American Gothic is the issue of race, the Native American Indians (who return in *Poltergeist*, 1982) and slavery (*Candyman*, 1992). The works of Edgar Allan Poe, representative of Southern Gothic, are most well known in American literature, and Roger Corman successfully adapted a number of his stories in the 1960s, including *The Raven* (1963) and *The Masque of the Red Death* (1964).

Se7en's Gothic belongs to the European tradition, which is drawn on through film noir and horror (see Genre). In Style we saw how the use of wide-angle lens distorts the setting and how John Doe's apartment is a 'perverted' space. The distortion acts to 'make strange' a familiar space, and Doe's religious haven suggests that terror can lurk behind the most innocuous wall (see also *Candyman*).

Se7en deals with the Seven Deadly Sins, a European creation, whose power has lapsed: they are repressed and 'silent' in secular society. As we saw in Narrative and Form: Theme, many of these Sins are no longer considered wrong. Doe's machinations, however, in turning the 'Sin' against the perpetrator, dramatise the *return* of the Seven Deadly Sins to modern society.

THE CITY

If we consider the opposition 'town versus country', we find that the former is usually associated with negative elements such as pollution, squalor and crime while the latter is deemed to be clean, natural and safe. The fact that these expectations are not always fulfilled matters little when we are considering modes of representation. Throughout film, and literature before it, the city has more often been associated with death and degradation whilst the countryside has signified a place of life and vigour.

One of cinema's early dystopias, a place where society has gone wrong, is featured in Lang's *Metropolis* (1926) while Scott's *Blade Runner* (1982, director's cut 1991) featured a hellish Los Angeles in 2019. Films noir are invariably set in the city (exceptions include *On Dangerous Ground*, 1951, and *Jennifer 8*, 1992), and *Se7en* follows generic convention in portraying an urban nightmare (though here the countryside is no better). *Se7en* also draws upon Christian mythology of the city:

> The single Christian poem which continues to shape our deep fantasies ... follows [the] strategy [of] using the City as the model or prototype of Hell: a symbol of alienation rather than fulfilment, of shared misery rather than communal bliss. In Dante's *Divine Comedy* ... Hell is a walled city.
>
> *Fiedler, 1981, p. 115*

Dante's *Divine Comedy, The Inferno,* is one of a number of texts (others being by Chaucer and Shakespeare) that Somerset uses to decipher Doe's *modus operandi*. Dante wrote *The Inferno* in the early fourteenth century after being exiled from Florence, then a city-state. The poem tells the fantastic tale of Dante, as an Everyman, being guided around Hell by the great Roman poet, Virgil. The characters they meet as they pass through the circles of Hell mostly relate to contemporaries of Dante and the poem reflects the author's embitterment at being exiled. To an extent, Somerset is Virgil to Mills's Dante as he guides the latter through the city. The words Dante's characters see inscribed about the 'portal's lofty arch' as they enter Hell, might serve as an epigraph for *Se7en*:

> Through me you pass into the city of woe:
> Through me you pass into eternal pain ...
> All hope abandon, ye who enter here.
>
> *Dante, 1998, p. 1 (Canto 3, lines 1, 2 and 9)*

cultural contexts

a place of woe

The city of *Se7en* is certainly a place of woe: it rains incessantly, murder is commonplace and Somerset believes that apathy reigns. It is an unnamed city, though actually filmed in Los Angeles, Philadelphia and New York (source: *www.imdb.com*). This is important at it suggests that the events portrayed could happen in any city, though the location is obviously North American.

Sociologists, such as Ferdinand Tönnies, have characterised recent social change as a migration from the countryside to the cities; in other words, the urbanisation of society. Tönnies's opposition of *Gemeinschaft* and *Gesellschaft* (roughly translated as 'community' and 'association') describes the rural 'community' as being based on living in small, intimate groups who supported one another; 'association', on the other hand, consists of impersonal and superficial relationships. The latter encourages alienation and an anomic form of existence:

> Whereas the social and physical spaces of pre-modern society formed an intimately related, lived totality, modernity brought about their colonization by a thoroughly *abstract* space, which ensured their fragmentation and disjunction.
>
> *Clarke, 1997a, p. 4*

It is in this 'abstract' space that the serial killer can easily thrive (see Serial killing below).

Although there is a long history of counter-pointing the pastoral setting of the 'natural' world with the man-made town, this has a particular resonance in North America. The nation had the status of being the New World (an Arcadia) and with this came the burden of utopian expectation. This was heightened by the myth of the pastoral. This view of America as having a 'moral geography' was most potently elucidated by Thomas Jefferson who believed that immersing oneself in America's wild landscape would allow the individual to 'emerge on a high plane of thought' (Slotkin, 1973, p. 247). North American literature, most famously in Thoreau's *Walden*, has drawn upon this tradition; in *Se7en* Mills characterises Somerset's cynicism as a belief that 'they should all go and live in a log cabin', figuratively Thoreau's

Walden. Significantly, Mills says 'I won't'. His refusal, the film suggests, destroys him.

In a scene deleted from the film, Somerset is shown visiting his retirement home in the country. He takes a piece of wallpaper back to the city as a memento. When he visits the Mills' home for a 'late supper', the wallpaper falls from his wallet and he discusses it with Tracy who says her husband won't understand what it means to Somerset. This helps explain why Tracy felt able to call Somerset to discuss her pregnancy. The absence of the scene in the country (it was an alternative opening) means we never see the countryside in a positive way. The high tension towers of the final scene scar the landscape, demonstrating that the city has even penetrated into the country (source: *www.plastic-iguana.com/cuttingroomfloor*).

SERIAL KILLING

Serial killers, the FBI tells us, must kill at least four people over a period of more than three days; massacres therefore do not count (Seltzer, 1998, p. 9). Serial killing, more or less, started in the twentieth century and, with some exceptions, is a white, male, western occupation. Their victims are usually women or socially subordinate men. Undoubtedly, then, it must be social in origin:

> Serial killing is often taken to be the crime of our age. It is held to be facilitated by the anonymity of mass societies and the ease and rapidity of modern transport, to be bred from the dissolution of the affective bonds of community and fomented by the routinisation of the sexual objectification of women in the media.
>
> *Dyer, 1997a, p. 14*

We touched upon the impersonality of the city above; in a small community it would be impossible for the killer to operate, as someone would know what he was doing. In addition to the anonymity the city provides, serial killers have chameleon-like abilities to merge with their

the desire to kill

landscape. The killers are normally motivated only by the desire to kill;
killing is sufficient in itself:

> ... murder retains the pure character of the *acte gratuite*. Which
> is one reason why murder, from DeQuincey and Poe on, has been
> aestheticized as one of the fine arts (murder for murder's sake).
>
> *Seltzer, 1998, p. 134*

It is possible that the extreme anonymity experienced by the killer may
be what leads him to kill, for in doing so he will become the object of
attention:

> On the one side, there is a location of identity in mass celebrity
> (the sheer *sociality* of the most-wanted man), and on the other,
> self-defense (*sic*) against the traumatic failure of self-distinction
> in the mass (the survivor's murderous *asociality*).
>
> *Ibid., p. 13*

Seltzer links serial killing to 'wound culture' which focuses upon trauma.
This trauma (which is the Greek word for wound) is not only bodily injury
(which the rubbernecking individuals seek to see after accidents) but also
the psychological trauma on display in talk shows, such as those of Jerry
Springer. The high ratings of such programmes, and the seemingly
inexhaustible supply of people willing to display their wounds, suggest
they play a significant role in our society. Serial killer films are part of this
wound culture.

genre

Se7en is a mix of a number of genres, including film noir, serial killer and
horror.

FILM NOIR

> It was during the summer of 1946 that French moviegoers
> discovered a new type of American film ... movies which shared

Film noir offers an
Expressionist look at reality.

Courtesy of Columbia Pictures

the hard-boiled detective narrative

> a strange and violent tone, tinged with a unique kind of
> eroticism: ... *The Maltese Falcon*, ... *Laura*, ... *Murder, My Sweet*, ...
> *Double Indemnity*, and ... *The Woman in the Window*.
>
> Borde and Chaumeton, 1999, p. 17; first published in 1955

Deprived of Hollywood movies during the German occupation of the
Second World War, French critics had the opportunity, after the war's
end, to view a glut of movies made during the war years. They saw a
group of films that had a visual style in common and narratives that
shared the mood of *serie noire* novels. They dubbed these film noir and a
new genre was born.

The fact that the makers of these movies were not aware of the existence
of film noir is not important. The *zeitgeist* ('spirit of the times') of 1940s'
North America, plus changing conditions of film production and the
influx of many German émigrés, laid the foundation for the new genre.

Although there are disputes as to which film qualifies as the first film
noir, many critics cite the John Huston-directed *The Maltese Falcon*
(1941) as the ground-breaking movie. Based on Dashiel Hammet's novel,
and featuring private detective Sam Spade, *The Maltese Falcon* had the
hard-boiled detective narrative that was characteristic of pulp fiction
that thrived, in the 1920s, as serials in magazines such as *Black Mask*. It
was not until three years later, with the arrival of the other films cited
above by Borde and Chaumeton, that the classic film noir cycle got into
full flow, culminating with *Touch of Evil* in 1958. The hiatus, between
1941 and 1944, was probably a result of Hollywood responding to the
war effort.

Unsurprisingly, the Second World War caused massive social upheaval,
possibly most lastingly felt in the changing role of women. As men
fought on the front line, women were drafted into factories to take on
'men's' work. This gave women a sense of independence and helped fuel
their husbands'/boyfriends' fantasies about what 'their' women might be
up to. In addition, at the war's end, men wanted 'their' jobs back and
women were forced back into the home or the menial employment they
had 'enjoyed' before the war. This eruption of gender identity was
expressed in the film noir character of the *femme fatale*.

angles that made the 'normal' grotesque

In addition, many soldiers were traumatised by their wartime experiences. They had spent up to five years fighting in the company of men and killing in terrifying conditions, so the return to civilian life was anything but easy. Many suffered from the then largely unrecognised post-traumatic stress syndrome. Hence many film noir characters are veterans, suspicious of women, psychologically scarred by their experiences and capable of psychotic violence.

Also during the 1940s, the theories of psychoanalyst Sigmund Freud became fashionable in North America. His belief that human beings' civilised nature was barely skin deep and our 'animal side', the id, was never far away can be seen in film noir's narratives that investigate the dark side of humanity.

Paul Kerr (1999) has suggested that industrial constraints helped fuel the film noir genre. These films were made as B pictures (as distinct from the prestigious and expensive A pictures) and were made on tight schedules with little interference from the studio producer. This relative independence meant experimentation was possible in both visual style and narrative. With the time constraints (Edgar Ulmer's classic *Detour*, 1945, was made in *six* days), night and location shooting were required, which helped in the development of film noir's look.

The influx of German directors, who were fleeing the Nazis, was probably most influential. During the early 1920s, a number of German films drew upon the Expressionist visual style that emphasised characters' state of mind by exaggerating and distorting the exterior world. In film noir, this mutated into lighting patterns that used shadows to distort people and objects, and camera angles that made the 'normal' grotesque. This visual style can be considered to be the **iconography** of film noir; indeed some critics argue that film noir is not a genre at all but a film movement characterised by its visual style (see Place, 1980). Westerns, such as *Rancho Notorious* (1952), have been shot as film noir. *Rancho Notorious* was directed by Fritz Lang, who made his name in Germany with films like *Metropolis* (1927) and *M* (1931). Lang made many classic films noir, including *Woman in the Window* and *The Big Heat* (1953). As we saw in Background: Director as auteur, Lang has influenced David Fincher.

no hope for modern society

Although critics suggest the classic film noir cycle ended in 1958, films noir continued to be made: *Odds Against Tomorrow* was released in 1959 and *Cape Fear* three years later. However, it was not until the 1980s that there appeared a large number of films that shared film noir characteristics and these have been dubbed *neo noir*. *Body Heat* (1981) possibly heralded this return to favour of the convoluted narrative dealing with corrupt individuals. As a 1980s' remake of *Double Indemnity*, the sex scenes in *Body Heat* could be as explicit as those in the earlier film noirs had been implicit.

A number of *neo noirs*, including *Chinatown* (1974) and *L.A. Confidential* (1997), can be considered as pastiches that knowingly, and lovingly, recreate the style of earlier films, albeit in colour and with a modern sensibility. Other *neo noirs*, such as *Se7en*, move the genre forward and so avoid pastiche. *Se7en*'s unmitigated tale of woe (most classic films noir did at least gesture toward a happy ending), suggests there is little, or no hope for modern society (see Critical Responses).

There is not enough space here to do justice to the variations and complexity of film noir; for a more in-depth, though still relatively brief survey, see Lacey (2000) or any of the following books dedicated to the genre: Cameron (1992), Hirsch (1999), Kaplan (1980) or Krutnik (1991).

SERIAL KILLER FILMS

The serial killer movie is probably not a genre in itself, but a sub-genre of the 'cop film'. The cop movie usually focuses on the apprehension of a criminal and differs from the characteristic film noir in that the protagonists are representatives of the discourse of law. The film noir's private eye is just that, an individual with – invariably – his own agenda. Serial killers, by their very nature, require the forces of law and order to pursue them – though *Kalifornia* (1993) – which featured Brad Pitt as a serial killer (the 'white trash' Early Grayce) – is an exception. Grayce, though, has no *modus operandi*, he simply kills people who dare to get in his way.

One of the difficulties that the detectives have in apprehending the serial killer is the enigma of the killer's motivation. While, in reality, the

war makes serial killers of its soldiers

motivation is the killing itself, in film the narrative usually offers a pattern to the killer's behaviour. Sometimes the serial killing may be a smokescreen, as in the French film *The Sleeping Car Murders* (1965), where the inhabitants of a sleeping car are all murdered to disguise the motive for the killing of one person.

In *The Name of the Rose* (1986), however, a pattern was found by the protagonist. The Holmesian William of Baskerville (Sean Connery) discovered the killer was attempting to suppress rational thought in favour of religion. As in *Se7en*, the killings are based on a religious text, the *Visions of the Apocalypse*. Luis Bunuel's serial killer movie, *The Criminal Life of Achibaldo de la Cruz* (1955), is bizarre in that the killer never actually kills any of his victims and so when he confesses to the police, he is, unsurprisingly, not believed.

Amongst the first serial killer characters in film was the somnambulist Cesare in the classic *The Cabinet of Dr Caligari* (1919). The film is remembered now as one of the few purely Expressionist films with totally non-naturalistic sets; even the shadows were painted.

> According to the pacifist-minded Janowitz [one of the scriptwriters], they had created Cesare with the dim design of portraying the common man who, under the pressure of compulsory military service, is drilled to kill ...
>
> *Kracauer, 1947, p. 65*

Made just after the end of the First World War, *The Cabinet of Dr Caligari* suggests that war makes serial killers of its soldiers.

Alfred Hitchcock's first great movie was based on the serial killer Jack the Ripper and has an evident debt to Expressionism (Hitchcock had worked at Ufa studios in Germany). The main character of *The Lodger* (1925) is mistaken for the killer, the Avenger, when he is actually pursuing the murderer after his sister had become a victim. However, although it appears that the Avenger is captured at the end, there remains an uncertainty (Richard Allen (1999a) calls it 'metaskepticism') as to whether the hero is in fact the villain. This lack of certainty about others is symptomatic of the anonymity provided by the city. Hitchcock's *Suspicion* (1941) takes this further by suggesting that we cannot even necessarily trust people we love.

Hitchcock made a number of serial killer movies, the most famous of which is *Psycho*. His own favourite film, however, was *Shadow of a Doubt* (1943) where small town American peace is shattered by the arrival of 'good ole Uncle Charlie'. He is visiting his niece after being burned out by his killing spree. Hitchcock's penultimate film, *Frenzy* (1972), features a famous shot when the camera, having followed the killer up a spiral staircase, returns 'alone' as the next victim is murdered. The movement plays with the audience's desire to see, denying us the 'satisfaction' of seeing another death. However, as the film includes a particularly grisly scene of rape and strangulation, most in the audience will be glad that the camera 'backs away'. In the rape scene:

> ... all attempts at seduction of the viewer are gone. No spectacular camera movements, no luxurious lighting, no glamorous movie stars. We are in a drab, straightforward universe in which all touch is violence ... all sex is rape, and human beings are reduced to a set of animal-like instincts and behaviour.
>
> McElhaney, 1999, pp. 98–9

Hitchcock draws attention to scopophilia, the pleasure we get from seeing. However, he takes this further by suggesting we question why we want to see terrible things. This voyeuristic impulse is also explored in *Peeping Tom* (1960). Indeed, so effectively did the director Michael Powell make the spectator feel bad about what he or she was seeing that he suffered extreme vilification at the hands of critics and never made another film. *Peeping Tom* is a self-reflexive serial killer film; that is, it deals with the subject of film making, as well as that of murder.

The Eyes of Laura Mars (1978) also deals with spectatorship and serial killing; however, its treatment of the subject is exploitative. Laura Mars is a photographer whose vision is unknowingly inspired by police

women who sexually arouse are despatched

crime-scene photographs. She can also 'see' what the killer sees as he attacks his next victim. It could be argued that the film is trying to make a statement about the sexual objectification of women and male insecurity:

> ... through its choice of the killer's particular crime, the film alludes to man's horror of the woman, who reverses the dynamics of vision, who dares to look back.
>
> *Fischer, 1982, p. 12*

However, it can be argued that its statement about sexual politics is merely an excuse to show off the bodies of women and subject them to violence. It is a High Concept film (see Hollywood) – it foregrounds its use of pop music and photographer Helmet Newton's images – which collapses underneath its own weight of pretentiousness. Its misogynist stance is further emphasised by the fact that the killer is motivated by hatred of his mother. Similarly, in *Dressed to Kill* (1980), women who sexually arouse the killer are despatched. The subtext is that sexually assertive women should be punished.

Though *Henry, Portrait of a Serial Killer* (1985) was resolutely unexploitative in its treatment of material based on the killer Henry Lee Lucas, its release was delayed many years and the British Board of Film Classification cut it. Like *Peeping Tom, Henry, Portrait of a Serial Killer* made the killing uncomfortable for the audience rather than an entertaining spectacle. John McNaughton, the director of *Henry, Portrait of a Serial Killer*, draws attention to our voyeurism when Henry and his accomplice Otis watch a videotape of themselves committing murder:

> The most horrific moment is Otis' line, 'I want to watch it again', which leads him to reshow on frame-advance the sequence of images an audience must be relieved to think is over.
>
> *Newman, 1991, p. 44*

Henry is a particularly horrific killer because, like real-life killers, he has no motivation to kill, no grand plan or method, he simply enjoys it.

In 1992, the year after *Henry, Portrait of a Serial Killer* was belatedly released in Britain, serial killing got Oscar recognition with *The Silence of the Lambs* (1991). It gained a total of seven Academy Awards including the most prestigious of Best Picture, Best Director and Best Actor and Actress. This stamp of Academy approval was interesting for, as Carol Clover says, the film is 'high slasher' (Clover, 1992, p. 233) and belongs to the tradition of *Nightmare on Elm Street* (1984) and *Blood Feast* (1963). It could be argued that the high production values, and quality performances by Jodie Foster and Antony Hopkins in particular, are all that separate this film from low-budget shockers like Abel Ferrara's infamous *Driller Killer* (1979).

Ferrara has supplied us, in *Ms.45* (1981), with that rarity in real life, a female serial killer. *Ms.45* is a rape-revenge movie where Thana kills the second man who rapes her in the same day. She cuts up the body and then distributes it in bin bags throughout the city. When accosted again, she shoots her attacker with a .45 and this leads her on to a trail of vengeance, mostly against men who try and pick her up. In the end a woman, who holds the knife phallically, stabs her in the back. Although it may appear that *Ms.45* is progressive in the way a woman is seen to act in defence of herself, Carol Clover doubts this:

> At the very least, the male spectator may take some comfort (or sadistic delight?) in the idea that his services as protector of his wife or girlfriend are not as obligatory as an earlier era would have them be.
>
> Clover, 1992, p. 143

A serial killer film with a definite feminist agenda is *Blue Steel* (1990), directed by Kathryn Bigelow. Here the protagonist, Megan Turner, finds herself the object of the killer's obsession. However, Turner is a cop and so is not simply a victim but also an action hero. The film brilliantly articulates the battles a woman must fight in patriarchal society against, in the case of Turner, not only the killer but also her father and male colleagues.

the rational and the psycho

Basic Instinct (1992) has both a female serial killer and high production values. An erotic thriller, it posits a female character (Catherine Tramell played by Sharon Stone) so bored with life, and superior to the men around her, that she can only get her kicks by *apparently* killing whilst having sex. In order to help the hapless cops, led by Nick Curran (Michael Douglas), she writes what she is going to do in her novels. The film has been labelled misogynist (the infamous no-knickers scene) and homophobic: one of Tramell's lovers is a lesbian who tries to kill Curran. Although the film's final scene suggests the killer is Tramell, an ex-lover of Curran's had already been revealed as the murderer.

Basic Instinct is typical of Hollywood in that it does not have a coherent discourse. From one perspective, the character of Tramell is shown to be a powerful woman and Curran is not a typical hero: he virtually rapes his girlfriend. In addition, unlike the traditional *femme fatale*, Tramell is not 'punished' for her sexual assertiveness. Despite this, its objectification of the female body places it firmly within the patriarchal mainstream.

The very randomness of most serial killers makes their *modus operandi* a code that is very difficult to crack. Hence protagonists spend time trying to 'get into the mind of the killer'. This was explicitly the case in *Manhunter* (1986) and *The Cell* (2000).

There are basically two types of serial killers: the rational and the psycho. The former can be rational human beings, most obviously shown in the three Hannibal Lecter films, while the latter are little more than monsters (Early Grayce and Leatherface of *The Texas Chainsaw Massacre*, 1974). The killers also can be both: *Psycho's* Norman Bates is shy and inoffensive until riled by his 'mother'.

The Texas Chainsaw Massacre more properly belongs to the horror genre, but horror is an important ingredient of the serial killer movie. *The Bone Collector* (1999) goes as far as a mainstream movie can in suggesting the extreme ways the victims die. As we have seen, *Se7en* draws upon Joel-Peter Witkin's Gothic imagery for the staging of Doe's victims.

Many horror films ostensibly use serial killing as their basis: *Halloween* (1978) and the *Scream* series (1996–2000), for example. In some cases, such as the *Nightmare on Elm Street* series (1984–94), the killer has supernatural powers. In the *Scream* series, however, the killer apparently works within the normal rules of existence, give or take a contrived plot point or three. In these films, the emphasis is on the terror of the victim rather than the procedures of the detectives; the cop Dewey in the *Scream* series is played for laughs, the Neve Campbell character has to save herself. As we saw in Narrative and Form: Story & Plot, there are points in *Se7en* where it appears that Doe has supernatural powers, such is his ability to control events. This is appropriate given the film's religious underpinnings and although Doe is not the 'Devil himself', his diabolical machinations suggests that he is as near to it as a human can get. *Fallen* (1998), which is heavily indebted in theme and style to *Se7en*, mixes the supernatural horror discourse with the cop movie. Denzil Washington's John Hobbes is an angel who, like Mills, is trying to do good in the city. The city, however, is a place where it is easy for evil to move as is demonstrated in the scene where the demon transfers itself from one person to another in a crowded street as it pursues a victim. Like *Se7en*, this film concludes in the countryside and with despair.

Although serial killers are primarily motivated by a desire to kill, they usually also crave celebrity. Numerous films have played with this idea, most explicitly in *Natural Born Killers* (1994). This in itself makes serial killers a modern phenômenon, for without the mass media, celebrity is impossible. Doe's motivation is to hold a mirror up to 'a world this shitty', so no one will regard sin as 'trivial'; he wants to do something that will never be forgotten. Being the most wanted is an enormous change from being an undifferentiated individual in the masses (see also Serial Killing above). In *Badlands* (1974) (based on Charles Starkweather's 1958 killing spree), Kit (Martin Sheen) struts like James Dean after he has been caught and is treated with reverence by his captors.

Sympathy with the killers is rare, though Fritz Lang's *M* (1931), with Peter Lorre's *tour de force* performance, gives an insight into the demons that make him kill children. Significantly, the film finishes without us knowing what judgement is pronounced upon Hans Beckert (based on the Dusseldorf killer Peter Kurten). This suggests that maybe we have no right to judge when our mass culture is obsessed by serial killing. *Sliver*

violence as entertainment

(1993) rather bizarrely ends with the killer being ridiculed by the heroine's laughter; a response also present in *Copycat* (1995), but here the murderer is despatched with *élan* by the film's protagonist.

Clearly killers deserve little, or none, of our sympathy but a society that produces killers, which the USA seems particularly adept at doing, may well itself be sick in some way. Serial killer movies deal with people who are sick; however, what are we to make of the companies that make money out of serial killing? Why do we take pleasure in watching serial killing being rendered on the screen? *M* satirises the public's obsession with serial killing:

> The camera frames a police poster which reads "10 000 Marks Reward, Who is the Murderer?' It slowly pulls back, revealing adjacent posters advertising a boxing match, a comedy stage, a circus, a dance school and a movie theatre ... Serial murder had become part of mass culture, qualified to compete with nightly entertainment, with which it shares its serial nature.
>
> *Kaes, 2000, p. 38*

The serial killer movie *Funny Games* (1997) explicitly attacks the Hollywood notion of violence as entertainment. Director Michael Haneke's film is an exercise in psychological torture, of both the victims and the audience. We never see the police pursuing the killers, indeed they may not be doing so, as the next bourgeois family is toyed with before their deaths. This gives an entrapped feel to the narrative: we feel certain that the victims have no chance to escape and our only escape will be the end of the movie (or to leave *now*).

HORROR

The horror genre basically draws upon our fear of death and:

> ... the multiple ways in which it can occur, and the untimely nature of its occurrence. The central generic image of the corpse reminds the viewer of extinction.
>
> *Wells, 2000, p. 10*

the horror exists in the mind

Serial killing represents random and motiveless death that could happen to any one of us; *Se7en* adds the element of body horror with its aesthetic display of the corpses. Body horror focuses on trauma to the body and is relatively new to mainstream cinema. Luis Bunuel and Salvador Dali had, in *An Adalusian Dog*, enraged spectators with an eyeball slit by a razor blade in 1928. But up until the 1960s, a body's usual response to death was often little more than a twitch, a glazed look in the eyes followed by a collapse. However, the visceral horror of the slasher movie draws attention to the body's wounds that result in death. The 'exploding stomach' death endured by Kane in *Alien* (1979) is one of the most shocking examples of body horror; it also played with male fear of pregnancy. One of the reasons that body horror is so terrifying is because:

> [In] Christian heritage ... the body [is accorded] a very high place in the definition of human personality. It is precisely this stress on the body that makes the separation from it in death such a prospect of terror ...
>
> *Warner, 1985, p. 97*

The *Scream* series took great delight in the evisceration of its victims, something that its target audience (sixteen to twenty-five year olds with a male bias) seems to delight in. *Se7en* draws upon body horror, particularly in the grotesque Gluttony, the self-mutilation of Greed and the bodily degradation of Lust. However, it does not dwell upon this horror in an exploitative fashion. The camera 'looks away' for us relatively quickly and all death (even the moment of Doe's) happens off screen. In this way, and with the reference to Witkin's photography, the body horror is aestheticised. Those who wish to see lots of gore will not find it in this film. The horror exists in the mind of the audience as they consider the implications of what has happened.

Whilst the Lust body is probably the most viscerally horrific in the film, the shooting of Doe is probably the most psychologically terrifying. This horror is caused by tension created by the uncertainty of whether Mills will shoot or not, and in our identification with Mills and sorrow at his predicament.

hollywood

Hollywood makes movies to make money and this is done by entertaining audiences (see Audience). One of the ways in which Hollywood films have always entertained, as we saw in Narrative and Form: Story & Plot, is the 'happy ever after' conclusion. Since 1975, and the massive success of *Jaws*, the studios have commodified their films further through the development of the High Concept. While *Jaws* was not the first blockbuster, it did herald the beginning of the studios' reliance upon the *summer* blockbuster to bolster their profitability.

Before *Jaws*, films usually had a platform release, i.e. they would open first in the big cities before rolling out across the country. This allowed awareness to build over a number of weeks. *Jaws*, however, following the example of the re-release of *Billy Jack* (1971) two years earlier, had a blanket release in 409 cinemas simultaneously. Today this would not be described as a blanket release: the summer would-be blockbusters are released to over 3,000 screens. In 1975, however, this represented a new pattern of release.

By opening wide, the studio must rely upon marketing to build awareness, rather than word of mouth. By 2000, an average of around $25 million was spent on marketing films, half the average cost of the films. In order to facilitate this blanket marketing, films became increasingly made using the High Concept (see Wyatt (1994), Maltby (1998) and Lacey and Stafford (2000)). In brief, the High Concept is a film that can be described in twenty-five words or less. This means that the film's premise must be simple and easy to explain and thus straightforward to market. *Se7en* could be described as: 'Seven deadly sins: gluttony, greed, sloth, pride, lust, envy and wrath. Will the killer be caught before he finishes his seven murders?' This is summarised by one of the film's taglines: Seven deadly sins. Seven ways to die. Seven ways to kill.

There is more to the High Concept than simplicity. The movie is conceived in terms of how it will be marketed:

hollywood

■ Sequences will be included specifically to be used in film trailers and adverts

■ Music will be an integral part of the film so it can be used in music videos and in the soundtrack album

■ The look of the film will be glossy to emphasise the 'eye candy' nature of the blockbuster

■ Genre is used in as wide a sense as possible in order to appeal to a broad audience

■ Stars are used in a self-conscious fashion.

In addition, the High Concept movie is characterised by **postmodern** irony and allusions to other films and media texts.

In 2000, much of this could be seen in the trailer for *Mission: Impossible 2* where the star Tom Cruise hangs precariously above the Grand Canyon, one of the wonders of the world: audiences can ogle at both. One of the stunts we are shown is Cruise, apparently, doing a front-wheel wheelie on a motorbike; as he says, with postmodern playfulness on the soundtrack, 'You've gotta be kidding!' As a sequel, the movie is already pre-sold, just as was the original that was based on a television series. *Mission: Impossible 2*'s genre is action-adventure, but it also has elements of the spy movie and thriller.

The degree to which *Se7en* is a High Concept film is debatable. Certainly its narrative can be enticingly marketed; however, the plot itself is complex and does not deliver what audiences expect. The look of the film is striking but not in a glossy fashion; it is too dark to be attractive. It certainly mixes genres (see above), but uses its stars in a straightforward fashion; they stick to their personas without 'winking' to the audience in a postmodern way. However, the stars were used to sell the film and the Freeman-Pitt combination delivers what it promises.

Se7en's trailer is quite unusual as it does not simply throw in the best bits of the film. It is also well constructed as it is built around the theme of seeing. At the opening, Mills asks: 'Do you like what you do for a living ... These things you see?' At the end, he asks Somerset: 'Have you ever seen anything like this?' and receives the reply, 'Never'. For fans of film noir, a genre that promises to show what should not be seen by 'respectable society', this is enticement enough. The rapid cutting of the trailer also makes it difficult to see detail, but there is enough action included to reassure those who want visceral pleasure that the film has exciting scenes. The bleakness of the city runs throughout the trailer and in this does not try and offer High Concept gloss. One of the critics, cited in Background: Trailer, uses the term to mock the film and concludes it is 'MTV-bosh'. This critic clearly does not watch much MTV. *Se7en* has smatterings of the High Concept about it, but subverts the concept's sunny world view.

Se7en is more typical of Hollywood product in the way it was made. The history of the company that produced the film is typical of how Hollywood has evolved over the last thirty years. New Line Productions began life as a distributor in the 1960s with a mixture of arthouse (foreign movies by directors such as Pier Paolo Pasolini and Claude Chabrol) and exploitation movies (such as *The Texas Chainsaw Massacre*, 1974). By the late 1970s, competition in this sector of the market was intense and producers were starting to pre-sell their movies: that is, distributors were asked to stump up money before the film was made in order to have the right to distribute the film. This helped producers hedge against loss and more or less guaranteed distribution for their films. For distributors, buying into pre-production deals is only a small step to going into film production themselves.

This New Line did. Sticking to low-budget fare, it hit pay dirt with the *Nightmare on Elm Street* franchise that started in 1984. In 1990, the $135 million North American box office gross of *Teenage Mutant Ninja Turtles* made it, at the time, the most successful independently-produced movie ever made (Wyatt, 1998). A successful independent will attract a major corporation and in 1993 Turner Broadcasting Corporation merged with New Line. Turner wanted New Line's movie catalogue as material for his television stations. In 1996, Turner merged again, this time with Time-Warner, which merged with AOL in 2001. Somewhere in the mega-corporation, AOL-Time-Warner, New Line still makes movies. Even when part of a large corporation, New Line operates with a degree of autonomy which no doubt helped such a dark property as *Se7en* getting the green light.

Pitt's attachment to the project would also have been crucial. Pitt is an example of a new type of Hollywood star who will choose projects for their challenge as much as the money they will earn. The late 1990s may be seen as a golden age of Hollywood with such diverse fare as *Very Bad Things* (1998), *Fight Club* (1999), *Being John Malkovich* (1999), *Three Kings* (1999) and *Nurse Betty* (1999) hitting the screens. These movies boasted names that helped sell the movie to both the financial backers and audiences: Christian Slater, Cameron Diaz (twice), John Cusack, George Clooney and Morgan Freeman. Diaz and Clooney also starred in two of 2000's blockbusters, *The Perfect Storm* and *Charlie's Angels*, showing they are equally at home with art and commerce.

Typically, *Se7en*'s unexpected success spawned a number of imitators including those that were exploitative and those that developed the movie's world view. *Resurrection* (1999) simply repackaged the horror and forgot the need to offer a coherent narrative; *Fallen* (1998), on the other hand, developed *Se7en*'s metaphysical view by staging an actual battle between demons and angels on Earth.

Another of Andrew Kevin Walker's scripts (*Se7en* was his sensational debut) was filmed by Joel Schumacher as *8mm* (1999). It, too, dealt with things that should not be seen, in this instance snuff movies where people are killed for entertainment. Whilst the subversive elements of *Se7en* are present – the villain is shown to be a capitalist who commissions snuff movies because he can afford to do so – the cack-handed way the film is directed, and an awful performance from the usually reliable Nicolas Cage, destroy any credibility the script may have had otherwise.

production history

How did Hollywood come to make a movie where evil triumphs and good is virtually lost in the stinking morass of contemporary life? After reading the script, David Fincher called his agent:

the 'head in the box' ending

> 'This movie, are they going to make this? I mean, have you read this thing?' and he said, 'Yeah, I read it.' And I said, 'There's this fucking head in the box at the end, it's just amazing. Are they really going to do this?' And he said 'No, you've got the wrong draft.'

> *Salisbury, 1996, p.81*

So a happy accident led to Fincher seeing the 'correct' script first. If he had seen the revised version, it is much less likely that he would have been interested. Although the film's producer, Arnold Kopelson, was dead against the 'head in the box' ending, Fincher says the desire to make a movie that would not be forgotten was enough to persuade the producer to accept the downbeat ending. The studio head, Michael De Luca, was easier to persuade.

Kopelson is, essentially, a producer of mainstream films. His biggest hits include *The Fugitive* (1993) and *Outbreak* (1995) and he has produced a number of would-be blockbusters including the Arnold Schwarzenegger vehicle *Eraser* (1996) and *Fugitive* spin-off *US Marshals* (1998). He has, however, also produced two other movies to put alongside *Se7en* in terms of interest: *Falling Down* (1993) and *Mad City* (1997).

It was Brad Pitt who enabled the movie Walker originally envisaged to be made and prevented a last-minute rescue being tacked on, or having Tracy's head substituted by a dog's:

> Pitt [had] an insistence written into his contract, that ensured the original ending's survival.

> *Dyer, 1999, p. 21*

Bankrolled to the tune of $30 million, *Se7en* is a mid-budget movie for Hollywood. The incessant rain, which gives the film much of its moody film noir tone, was necessitated by the fact they only had Pitt for fifty-five days of shooting. For reasons of continuity, it was simpler to have it rain all the time rather than risk having it rain the one time it was not wanted. Although this was a practical decision, it does not detract from the aesthetic effect the rain has in the film.

audience

This subversive, edgy movie was made by a chance conjunction of the 'wrong' script, a great director and a star that was willing to take risks.

audience

Although it appears Hollywood may be becoming more daring in the product it makes, audiences do not seem willing to take on intellectual challenges. Neither *Fight Club* or *Three Kings* were a big financial success and although *Being John Malkovich* and *Nurse Betty* did relatively well at the box office, their total grosses are often beaten in summer blockbusters' first three days' takings.

Most audiences want entertainment and escapism for a couple of hours from their everyday lives. The question remains, however, where do audiences escape to? It certainly is not into the film. Richard Dyer suggested that entertainment offers an ideal world, a utopia, not in the sense of describing this world but:

> Rather the utopianism is contained in the feelings [the film] embodies. It presents ... what utopia would feel like rather than how it would be organized.
>
> *Dyer, 1992, p. 18*

Dyer described these feelings as energy, abundance, intensity, transparency and community. In brief, entertainment shows: vigorous action; sensuous reality with no scarcity; direct and authentic emotion; easy to understand relationships; a sense of togetherness. Whilst this framework is very useful in showing how many films are entertaining, it is interesting to consider how *Se7en*, which offers a dystopian vision, entertains its audience:

Energy

The film contains two action sequences: the discovery of Sloth and Mills's chase of Doe. Although these both end in failure, they are still exciting to watch. The rapid editing, narrative excitement ('are they going to catch the villain?') and dynamism of the sequences fit them squarely with the action genre that is so popular.

a subversive film that entertains

Abundance

Despite *Se7en*'s 'miserable' **mise-en-scène**, it remains a fascinating film to look at. So carefully have sets been designed, the film edited and the camera positioned, that it rewards repeated viewings. The darkness that prevents us from seeing much detail requires a second look for us to find there is much to see.

Intensity

This is particularly evident in the climax where, as noted in Narrative and Form: Theme, the audience is placed in Mills's position: what would you do if that happened to you? Mills's turmoil is evident by the way he pleads with Somerset to tell him 'it isn't so' and his pacing toward and away from Doe as he decides to kill, then not to kill. Intensity is also apparent in the visceral horror of the murders; this is most obviously experienced in the description of Lust and the appearance of Sloth.

Transparency

Se7en is a 'buddy movie', a sub-genre of the cop film, where the partners 'love' one another. The developing relationship between the protagonists is one of the pleasures of the film; we are invited to admire Mills's idealism and Somerset's wisdom, and together they would make a formidable team. Mills and Tracy's relationship is obviously one of deep love: they were childhood sweethearts; Tracy happily digs some sleep from her husband's eye before he goes to work.

Community

This is wholly absent from the film except in Somerset's valedictory words. All the film has to offer, in terms of hope, is that if people like Somerset 'stay around', then maybe the world will get better.

If *Se7en* were not entertaining, it would not have made so much money at the box office, but it does offer an unusual example of a subversive film that entertains. It has spawned a number of Internet pages, as has director David Fincher. Clearly for film fans, Fincher's movies' subversive take on the contemporary world offers intellectual nourishment as well as visceral entertainment.

critical responses

Foster Hirsch spends two pages celebrating the brilliance of *Se7en* only to conclude that the film is 'morally hollow' (Hirsch, 1999, p. 282). Amy Taubin is similarly ambivalent, calling the script 'tacky' but the movie 'great film-making' (Taubin, 1996, p. 23). Richard Dyer, however, is unequivocal:

> The film is a single-minded elaboration of a feeling that the world is beyond both redemption and remedy … It is a gripping story, but even more it is a landscape of despair, a symphony of sin.
>
> *Dyer, 1999, p. 78*

Both Hirsch and Taubin are enraptured by Fincher's direction and the set design. Taubin, however, is particularly dismissive about the 'puerile genre script' (Taubin, 1996, p. 24), which she says is:

> … pretentious, slipshod (you literally can see the *dénouement* coming from miles away) and … rightwing.
>
> *Ibid., p. 23*

As was discussed in Narrative and Form, part of the film's brilliance is the construction of the narrative and Taubin must be very gifted to see the *dénouement* so clearly. Her political critique, though, holds more force:

> In *Seven*, man is corrupt, and cities are cesspools of contagion, spreading sin faster then (*sic*) TB. Forget the inequities of class or race, we're all sinners, and urban blight is the Lord's *décor* for the gates of hell.
>
> *Ibid.*

By defining Sin as metaphysical, that is defined by God, the social roots of sinning are not explored. The film's view on the city, as a morass of destitution and alienation, is resolutely asocial. There is no exploration of the woman Mills bribes to testify she called the detectives to Doe's apartment. She is patently a drug addict who will not spend the money given to her, as Mills insists, on food. The corruption of the estate agent who hides the true location of the Mills' flat from the buyers is left 'as read' (that's what estate agents are like). What is lacking is a political dimension, apparent in both *The Game*'s and *Fight Club*'s critique of bourgeois existence. However, it is asking a lot of one film to deal with several discourses in a coherent way. Besides, Taubin's statement that *Se7en* is right wing is debateable.

As noted in Narrative and Form: Theme, most of the Sins are not considered as such today; they belong to a medieval view of morality. However, this medieval view still has resonance for some today, particularly for right-wing religious fanatics. So it could be argued that *Se7en* lines up the intolerant bigots with Doe and in this it is, in fact, a progressive film.

Paul Wells, situating the film as part of the horror genre, has a persuasive suggestion as to why *Se7en* is both bleak and massively successful:

> Horror has somehow become a 'friend'; so much so that audiences can accept the bleak ending of *Se7en* (1995), which refuses any notion of redemption from its apocalyptic tale of fundamentalist obsession involving the seven deadly sins. This is a mature vision which recognises that audiences have come to terms with the darkness at the heart of contemporary civilisation and can endure its less palatable outcomes.
>
> *Wells, 2000, p. 108*

Se7en is great film making: in the script, mise-en-scène, editing, soundtrack, cinematography and acting. It uses millions of capitalist dollars to make a subversive film suggesting that there is something fundamentally sick with society. It also made millions for those capitalists who backed the film; such is Hollywood.

bibliography

general film

Altman, Rick, *Film/Genre*, BFI, 1999
  Detailed exploration of the concept of film genre

Bordwell, David, *Narration in the Fiction Film*, Routledge, 1985
  A detailed study of narrative theory and structures

– – –, Staiger, Janet & Thompson, Kristin, *The Classical Hollywood Cinema: Film Style & Mode of Production to 1960*, Routledge, 1985; pbk 1995
  An authoritative study of cinema as institution, it covers film style and production

– – – & Thompson, Kristin, *Film Art*, McGraw-Hill, 4th edn, 1993
  An introduction to film aesthetics for the non-specialist

Branson, Gill & Stafford, Roy, *The Media Student's Handbook*, Routledge, 2nd edn 1999

Buckland, Warren, *Teach Yourself Film Studies*, Hodder & Stoughton, 1998
  Very accessible, it gives an overview of key areas in film studies

Cook, Pam & Bernink, Mieke (eds), *The Cinema Book*, BFI, 2nd edn 1999

Corrigan, Tim, *A Short Guide To Writing About Film*, HarperCollins, 1994
  What it says: a practical guide for students

Dyer, Richard (with Paul McDonald), *Stars*, BFI, 2nd edn 1998
  A good introduction to the star system

Easthope, Antony, *Classical Film Theory*, Longman, 1993
  A clear overview of writing about film theory

Hayward, Susan, *Key Concepts in Cinema Studies*, Routledge, 1996

Hill, John & Gibson, Pamela Church (eds), *The Oxford Guide to Film Studies*, Oxford University Press, 1998
  Wide-ranging standard guide

Lapsley, Robert & Westlake, Michael, *Film Theory: An Introduction*, Manchester University Press, 1994

Maltby, Richard & Craven, Ian, *Hollywood Cinema*, Blackwell, 1995
  A comprehensive work on the Hollywood industry and its products

Mulvey, Laura, 'Visual Pleasure and Narrative Cinema' (1974), in *Visual and Other Pleasures*, Indiana University Press, Bloomington, 1989
  The classic analysis of 'the look' and 'the male gaze' in Hollywood cinema. Also available in numerous other edited collections

Nelmes, Jill (ed.), *Introduction to Film Studies*, Routledge, 2nd edn 1999
  Deals with several national cinemas and key concepts in film study

Nowell-Smith, Geoffrey (ed.), *The Oxford History of World Cinema*, Oxford University Press, 1996
  Hugely detailed and wide-ranging with many features on 'stars'

Thomson, David, *A Biographical Dictionary of the Cinema*, Secker & Warburg, 1975
Unashamedly driven by personal taste, but often stimulating

Truffaut, François, *Hitchcock*, Simon & Schuster, 1966, rev. edn. Touchstone, 1985
Landmark extended interview

Turner, Graeme, *Film as Social Practice*, 3rd edn, Routledge, 1999
Chapter four, 'Film Narrative', discusses structuralist theories of narrative

Wollen, Peter, *Signs and Meaning in the Cinema*, BFI 1997 (revised edn)
An important study in semiology

Readers should also explore the many relevant websites and journals. *Film Education* and *Sight and Sound* are standard reading.

Valuable websites include:

The Internet Movie Database at www.uk.imdb.com

Screensite at www.tcf.ua.edu/screensite/contents.html

The Media and Communications Site at the University of Aberystwyth at www.aber.ac.uk/~dgc/welcome.html

There are obviously many other university and studio websites which are worth exploring in relation to film studies.

se7en

Allen, Richard & Gonzales, S. Ishii (eds), *Alfred Hitchcock Centenary Essays*, BFI, 1999

Allen, Richard, 'Hitchcock, or The Pleasures of Metaskepticism', in *Alfred Hitchcock Centenary Essays*, Allen & Gonzales (eds), BFI, 1999a

Borde, Raymond & Chaumeton, Etienne (eds), *Towards a Definition of Film Noir*, Silver & Ursini, Limelight Editions, 1999

Bordwell, David & Thompson, Kristin, *Film Art*, 4th edn, McGraw-Hill, 1993

Cameron, Ian (ed.), *The Movie Book of Film Noir*, Studio Vista, 1992

Carroll, Peter N. & Noble, David W., *The Free and the Unfree, A New History of the United States*, Penguin Books, 1977

Clarke, David B. (ed.), *The Cinematic City*, Routledge, 1997

Clarke, David B., 'Introduction, Previewing the Cinematic City', in *The Cinematic City*, Clarke (ed.), Routledge, 1997a

Clover, Carol, *Men Women and Chainsaws, Gender in the Modern Horror Film*, BFI, 1992

Dante, Alighieri, *The Inferno*, Wordsworth Editions, 1998

Dyer, Richard, *Only Entertainment*, Routledge, 1992

Dyer, Richard, 'Is the camera racist?', in *The Guardian Friday Review*, 18 July 1997

Dyer, Richard, 'Kill and Kill Again', in *Sight and Sound*, vol. 7 issue 9, September 1997a

Dyer, Richard, *Seven*, BFI, 1999

Fiedler, Leslie, 'Mythicizing the City', in *Literature and the American Urban Experience, Essays on the City and Literature*, Jaye & Watts (eds), Manchester University Press, 1981

Fischer, Lucy, 'The Eyes of Laura Mars, A Binocular Critique', in *Screen*, vol. 23, nos 3–4, Sept/Oct 1982

Franks, Alan, 'Freakshow', in *The Sunday Times Magazine*, 14 March 1999

Goddu, Teresa A., *American Gothic, Narrative, History and Nation*, Columbia University Press, 1997

Gramsci, Antonio, *A Gramsci Reader*, David Forgacs (ed.), Lawrence & Wishart, 1988

Gunning, Tom, *The Films of Fritz Lang, Allegories of Vision and Modernity*, BFI, 2000

Hirsch, Foster, *Detours and Lost Highways, A Map of Neo-Noir*, Limelight Editions, 1999

Jackson, Rosemary, *Fantasy, The Literature of Subversion*, Methuen, 1981

Jaye, Michael C. & Watts, Ann Chalmers (eds), *Literature and the American Urban Experience, Essays on the City and Literature*, Manchester University Press, 1981

Kaes, Anton, *M*, BFI, 2000

Kaplan, E. Ann (ed.), *Women in Film Noir*, revised edn, BFI, 1980

Kerr, Paul, *Out of the Past? Notes on the B film noir*, Silver & Ursini (eds), Limelight Editions, 1999

Kracauer, Siegfried, *From Caligari to Hitler, A Psychological History of the German Film*, Princeton University Press, 1947

Krutnik, Frank, *In a Lonely Street, film noir, genre, masculinity*, Routledge, 1991

Lacey, Nick, *Narrative and Genre*, Palgrave, 2000

Lacey, Nick & Stafford, Roy, *Film As Product in Contemporary Hollywood*, BFI, 2000

Maltby, Richard, 'Nobody knows everything: post-classical historiographies and consolidated entertainment', in Neale, Steve & Smith, Murray (eds), *Contemporary Hollywood Cinema*, Routledge, 1998

McElhaney, Joe, 'Touching the Surface, *Marnie*, Melodrama, Modernism', in *Alfred Hitchcock Centenary Essays*, Allen & Gonzales (eds), BFI, 1999

Neale, Steve & Smith, Murray (eds), *Contemporary Hollywood Cinema*, Routledge, 1998

Newman, Kim, 'Henry, Portrait of a Serial Killer', in *Sight and Sound*, vol. 1 issue 3, July 1991

Place, Janey, in *Women in Film Noir*, Kaplan, E. Ann (ed.), revised edn, BFI, 1980

Pulver, Andrew, 'Fight the good fight', in *Guardian Friday Review*, 29 October 1999

Salisbury, Mark, 'Seventh Hell', in *Empire*, no. 80, February 1996

Seltzer, Mark, *Serial Killers, Death and Life in America's Wound Culture*, Routledge, 1998

Shohat, Ella & Stam, Robert, *Unthinking Eurocentrism, Multiculturalism and the Media*, Routledge, 1994

Silver – Wyatt

Silver, Alain & Ursini, James (eds), *Film Noir Reader*, Limelight Editions, 1999

Slotkin, Richard, *Regeneration Through Violence, The Mythology of the American Frontier, 1600–1860*, Wesleyan University Press, 1974

Taubin, Amy, 'The Allure of Decay', in *Sight and Sound*, vol. 6, no. 1, January 1996

Tönnies, Ferdinand, *Community and Society/Gemeinschaft Und Gesellschaft*, Transaction Publishers Paperback, 1988

Warner, Marina, *Alone of All Her Sex, The Myth and the Cult of the Virgin Mary*, Picador, 1985

Wells, Paul, *The Horror Genre, From Beezlebub to Blair Witch*, Wallflower Press, 2000

Withall, Keith, 'Into the Labyrinth – The Serial Killer Cycle', in *Film Reader 1*, In The Picture Publications, 1996

Wyatt, Justin, *High Concept, Movies and Marketing in Hollywood*, University of Texas Press, 1994

Wyatt, Justin, 'The formation of the 'major independent', Miramax, New Line and the New Hollywood', in *Contemporary Hollywood Cinema*, Neale, Steve & Smith, Murray (eds), Routledge, 1998

cinematic terms

auteur the theory that suggests the director can be considered to be the film's author (auteur)

blocking the positioning of actors in relation to one another and the camera

dissolve a type of edit – the transition between one shot and another – where the second shot fades in as the first fades out. They are both momentarily visible to the audience

dollies moves smoothly on tracks towards, or away from, the camera shot's subject

eyeline match an edit that creates a point of view shot by having a shot of a character looking at something immediately followed by what they are looking at (see point of view shot)

hegemony from Gramsci, the suggestion that the dominant groups retain their power through the consent of those who are subordinate

iconography significant visual or aural signs associated with particular genres

mise-en-scène what is 'in the picture' of the film's frame. This includes the position of objects and characters, the lighting of the scene and focus

montage a sequence of images that are not positioned together in narrative space but signify something particular, such as a journey

point of view shot a shot that is clearly from the point of view of a character. It is usually preceded by a shot of the character looking (see eyeline match)

postmodern/postmodernism an aesthetic that favours surface gloss over depth and intertextual references which simply refer to other texts without adding meaning

wipe an edit that moves across the screen from the edges like a curtain being drawn

credits

production company
New Line

director
David Fincher

executive producers
Gianni Nunnari, Dan Kolsrud and Anne Kopelson

producers
Arnold Kopelson and Phyllis Carlyle

screenplay
Andrew Kevin Walker

director of photography
Darius Khondji

editor
Richard Francis-Bruce

production design
Michael Kaplan

music
Howard Shore

visual effects
supervisor: Greg Kimple
co-ordinator: Tim Thompson

art director
Gary Wissner

production designer
Arthur Max

set design
Elizabeth Lapp, Lori Rowbathom and Hugo Santiago

special make-up effects
Rob Bottin

cast
Mills – Brad Pitt
Somerset – Morgan Freeman
John Doe – Kevin Spacey
Tracy – Gwyneth Paltrow
Talbot – Richard Roundtree
Police Captain – R. Lee Ermey
California – John C. McGinley
Mrs Gould – Julie Araskog
Greasy FBI Man – Mark Boone Junior
Officer Davis – John Cassini
Dr Santiago – Reginald E. Cathey
Dr O'Neill – Peter Crombie
Crazed Man in Massage Parlour – Leland Orser